HOW TO KEEP LAUGHING

EVEN THOUGH YOU'VE CONSIDERED ALL THE FACTS

by Richard Deats

FELLOWSHIP PUBLICATIONS
NYACK, NEW YORK

FELLOWSHIP PUBLICATIONS
Published by the Fellowship of Reconciliation
P.O. Box 271, Nyack, New York 10960-0271
fellowship@forusa.org

First printing 1994
Second printing 1999

ISBN 0-97409-720

Printed in the United States of America by
Allen Press, Inc.
Lawrence, Kansas

Typography and Design by Melinda Moore,
M Space Type & Design, New York, NY

To order directly from the publisher, add $2.75 for postage to the price for
up to two copies; add $4.50 for up to six copies. Send check or money
order to: **Fellowship Publications**, Box 271, Nyack, NY 10960

Printed on recycled paper

Dedicated to my father-in-law

❧ *Rex Baggett* ❧

*who always had a funny story to tell,
even during his final years suffering from emphysema.
His gentleness and humor brought joy to all who knew him.
His stories still enliven family gatherings.*

ACKNOWLEDGEMENTS

The title for this book was suggested by these lines from my favorite poet, Wendell Berry:

> *Laughter is immeasurable. Be joyful*
> *though you have considered all the facts.*

from "Manifesto: The Mad Farmer Liberation Front," p. 152 in Berry's *COLLECTED POEMS. 1957-1982.* San Francisco: North Point Press, 1985. Copyright Wendell Berry. Used by permission.

MOLLY IVINS CAN'T SAY THAT, CAN SHE? by Molly Ivins/ Peter Osnes, editor. New York: Random House, 1991. Copyright Molly Ivins. Used by permission.

"Speaking Out: In the Midst of Death, A Festival of Life" by Patricia Helman. Copyright Christian Century Foundation. Reprinted by permission from the March 23-30, 1983 issue of *The Christian Century.*

"The Joyful Noiseletter" (April 1991) The Fellowship of Merry Christians (P.O. Box 895, Portage, MI 49081-0895). Used by permission.

SOVIET LAUGHTER, SOVIET TEARS by Christine and Ralph Dull. Englewood, Ohio: Stillmore Press, 1992. Copyright Christine and Ralph Dull. Used by permission.

"Toys in My Attic" by Joseph Epstein. *The American Scholar,* Vol. 61. No. 1, Winter 1992. Copyright 1991 by the author. Reprinted by permission.

"Nigger" by Dick Gregory. New York, Washington Square Press Publication of Pocket Books, 1986. Copyright Dick Gregory.

Many persons have shared stories and jokes with me. I am especially indebted to Jim and Nancy Forest, Diana and Nico Francis, Naomi Goodman, Jo Clare Hartsig, Glenn Smiley, Melinda Moore, Glen Anderson, Stefan Merken, Paul Schilling, Ron Beasley, Jerry and Jo Anderson, Kathy and Dale Bruner, and Don Irish.

Special thanks go to Jim Shields, close friend since seminary days in Dallas, whose encouragement and generosity made this book possible.

TABLE OF CONTENTS

࿐ ࿐ ࿐ ࿐ ࿐ ࿐ ࿐ ࿐ ࿐ ࿐

HOW TO
KEEP LAUGHING

❧❧❧

EVEN THOUGH
YOU'VE CONSIDERED
ALL THE FACTS

INTRODUCTION

I was a pre-med student in college but about my junior year I decided to go to seminary instead of medical school. When I told my parents of my decision, they were shocked. They recounted the many ways they saw that as an unwise decision. Finally, my mother gave the clinching argument. "You can't be a minister," she said. "You have too much fun in life." Her stereotype was the all too common one of joyless, guilt-full religion. A priest once said to Groucho Marx, "Groucho, I want to shake your hand for all the joy you have brought into the world." Groucho responded, "Thank you, father. And I want to shake your hand – for all the joy you have taken out of the world."

Religion is serious but it is not joyless. The religious quest for meaning and fulfillment and the building of a just and decent society include the joyful celebration of life and the ability to laugh even in the midst of tragedy and suffering. Indeed, when one cannot see the humor in the face of life's foibles and paradoxes, one might easily give in to despair and bitterness. Laughter can keep you sane. In China the Methodist missionary Olin Stockwell was arrested and thrown in prison after the communist revolution, charged with being a Western spy. Reflecting on those years of isolation, he later wrote that the only thing that kept him going was "the grace of God and a sense of humor." A similar note was struck in Langdon Gilkey's *Shantung Compound*, the story of a Japanese internment camp during World War II. He tells the story of two interned Trappist monks who knelt to pray facing the stone wall that surrounded the compound. Through a hole in the wall they received eggs from farmers on the other side as they prayed, hiding the precious eggs under their robes and sharing them with the other inmates when the guards were not around. Finally they were caught – and as punishment, were placed in solitary confinement! How could the Japanese have known that Trappist monks spend their lives in solitude? The two monks and the other inmates were delighted at the unintended humor of an otherwise grim situation.

A sense of humor softens the blows of life and makes them more endurable. As Stefan Merken put it, "Humor is the basis of repair, not only of broken hearts but of shattered emotions. Without it, you die." "Laughter," says Joan Chittister, "makes the seriousness of life bearable, makes it transparent, makes it to size." Humor expresses a certain playful, whimsical approach to life, whatever happens to us. It brings an unexpected reversal of traditional categories and practices. In the Gospel accounts of Jesus' teachings, we are told that the first shall be last and the last shall be first. The one who exalts himself will be humbled. It is the poor, the meek, the merciful, the persecuted who are blessed. When you have a feast, you are to go out into the highways and hedges and invite the forgotten ones – the blind, the poor, the lame. When you set aside pride and become as a little child, you enter the Realm of Heaven. Garrison Keillor says, "Humor is not a trick, not jokes. Humor is a presence in the world – like grace – and shines on everybody." This grace-full presence makes for a better world. Richard Pryor observed, "I am proud that, like Mark Twain, I have been able to use humor to lessen people's hatred." It is said that two of the questions asked by Osiris of the Egyptians of antiquity seeking a peaceful eternity were: "Did you give joy?" and "Did you receive joy?" One of the most popular authors of children's books was Dr. Seuss. His nonsensical, whimsical stories have brought laughter to a whole generation of children – and their parents. Why did the Grinch steal Christmas, that time of great joy? Dr. Seuss muses:

> *the most likely*
> *reason of all*
> *may have been*
> *that his heart*
> *was two sizes too small.*

A few years back the musical "Godspell" portrayed the Messiah as a clown. And there have developed in our day growing numbers of people who see "clowning" as a vital part of ministry. Throwing off inhibition and donning a clown costume, they go into nursing homes and malls and churches and temples to help people laugh and learn to delight in life's playful, whimsical, paradoxical aspects.

In our own day there is increasing realization that humor is good for one's health. Oh, we always knew, as the book of Proverbs (17:22) put it: "A cheerful heart is good medicine." But this is being confirmed today by the medical profession. All too many doctors still tend to confine themselves to either cutting you up or filling you with antibiotics, period. But, thank God, growing numbers of them are beginning to see the human body and psyche in a more holistic way. In doing so they are discovering the importance of humor. Dr. Patch Adams, founder of the Gesundheit Institute, is one of the leaders in this approach. Norman Cousins, suffering from a severe illness – a crippling disease called ankylosing spondylitis – was unable to find relief and healing in the traditional medical approach. His condition worsened until he took his case in his own hands. He prescribed humor for himself, believing that laughter was indeed good, curative "medicine." He watched old movies of Laurel and Hardy and the Marx Brothers and videos of "Candid Camera." And his "medicine" worked: he got well! In his best seller, *Anatomy of an Illness*, he reported that laughter brought him a decrease in crippling inflammation, enhanced sound sleep and increased his well-being. In time, he was healed. Cousins refers to laughter as a kind of 'internal jogging' that should be undertaken on a regular basis. *Anatomy of an Illness* opened many doors for Cousins and he developed a whole new career lecturing on this alternative vision of well-being; eventually he joined the staff of the UCLA Medical School, where he continued to study the role of the mind and spirit in healing, while passing along his own insights.

Increasingly we are finding that laughter is indeed good for the body and for one's health. As Natalie Angier reported in *The New York Times*, "Scientists suspect that sensations like optimism, curiosity, rapture – the giddy, goofy desire to throw wide your arms and serenade the sweetness of spring – not only make life worth living, but also make life last longer. They think that euphoria unrelated to any ingested substance is good for the body, that laughter is protective against the corrosive impact of stress, and that joyful people outlive their bilious, whining counterparts." Or, as Mac Caldwell put it, "The surly bird gets the germ." Now that is good news! And it is beginning to show up in unexpected and exciting ways. For instance, there are now some hospitals and nursing homes that have humor rooms and humor carts with joke books, toys, tapes, and things that will amuse the patients. In Houston, the nuns at St. Joseph's Hospital are expected to tell each patient a funny story daily. At Oregon's Health Sciences University, there is a group called Nurses for Laughter. They wear buttons that say, "Warning: Humor May Be Hazardous to Your Health," although the opposite is true. There are now laughter therapy groups for cancer patients and doctors like Bernie Siegel, who strongly emphasize the therapeutic value of humor. Even if we fail to get well, humor still makes the pain more bearable and enhances one's well-being. A cherished friend, Ermelinda Quiambao, took a copy of this book to her chemotherapy sessions to help strengthen her immune system.

In Big Spring, Texas where I grew up, a local undertaker named Coy Nalley had an irrepressible urge to get people to laugh. When he visited someone in the hospital, he would walk into the patient's room, and solemnly pull out a tape measure. Without saying a word, he would write down the length and width of the patient. The ensuing laughter was the best gift he could have brought.

The award-winning movie, "Life is Beautiful", moved audiences to tears and laughter as it portrayed Guido, an irrepressible Italian Jew who ended up in a Nazi concentration camp with his little boy. Even in the midst of tragedy and suffering, Guido found ways of expressing his joyous unpredictable spirit.

How to Keep Laughing Even Through You've Considered All the Facts is hopefully a contribution to the world's joy. It is full of true funny things that have happened, as well as tall tales, favorite jokes, puns and spoonerisms. As with so much humor, the original source may be unknown: something funny is heard and it spreads like wildfire, especially since the advent of the internet and the e-mailing of jokes and humorous sayings. When I know the source, I gratefully mention where it comes from; often though I've no idea who first said it: I heard it, it lodged in my brain and now I share it with you. Whoever you are and whatever state you are in, I hope you have as much fun reading this as I did putting these recollections down on paper. Enjoy!

Richard L. Deats

*The creator made the
human able to do everything
– talk, run, look and hear.*

*The creator was not satisfied,
though, till the human could
do just one thing more,
and that was laugh.*

*And so the human laughed
and laughed and laughed.*

*And the creator said,
"Now you are fit to live."*

– APACHE MYTH

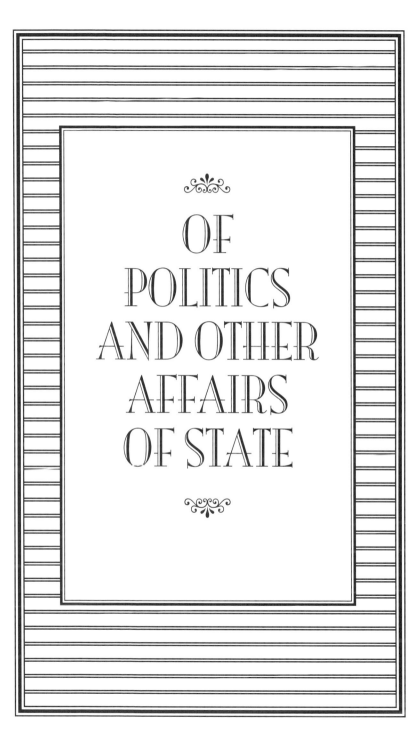

OF POLITICS AND OTHER AFFAIRS OF STATE

OF POLITICS AND OTHER AFFAIRS OF STATE

❧ ❧ ❧ ❧ ❧ ❧ ❧ ❧ ❧ ❧ ❧ ❧

In the world of politics and the affairs of nations, there are often humorous stories and quips, as well as things said unintentionally that provide great hilarity. Other stories about the famous and powerful help cut through the cant and pomposity of high public office. Here are a few of my favorites, some going back many, many years:

Abraham Lincoln, of course, was one of the great humorists and storytellers of the last century. He liked to tell the story of the woman who stared at him on the train and finally said, "You are the ugliest man I have ever seen in my life." "Well," said Lincoln, "I don't know what I can do about it." "You could stay home!" the woman replied. When he was President, someone asked him for a job. "I'm sorry," he said, "but I don't have any influence on this Administration."

☞

A distant relative of my wife was the famous Methodist frontier preacher, Peter Cartright. Cartright ran for Congress against Abe Lincoln. Once Cartright was preaching when he saw Lincoln come into the sanctuary and sit at the back. Cartright asked all who were going to heaven to raise their hands. Everyone did except Lincoln. "And where are you going?" Cartright asked Lincoln. Lincoln replied, "I'm going to Congress, Mr. Cartright." And he did, handily beating Cartright in the race.

Lincoln asked, "If you call a tail a leg, how many legs does a dog have? Four, because calling a tail a leg doesn't make it so."

Mark Twain said, "There is no distinctly criminal class in America except for Congress."

John Stuart Mill said, "Although it is not true that all conservatives are stupid,. it is true that most stupid people are conservative."

A congressional enemy of Teddy Roosevelt said, "The president has no more respect for the Constitution than a tom cat has for a marriage license."After World War I, wags said of President Woodrow Wilson's fourteen point peace program, "God had only ten commandments, Wilson has fourteen."

Will Rogers said, "Calvin Coolidge didn't do nothin' but that's what we wanted done." During the Depression, Rogers said, "The United States is the only country in the world that went to the poor house in an automobile."

Will Rogers was a good friend of Ft. Worth's Amon Carter. When Rogers was in Washington, Carter said he would introduce him to President Calvin Coolidge, renown as a taciturn man who rarely laughed. Carter and Rogers had a $50 wager on whether or not Rogers could make the president laugh.

Upon entering the White House Coolidge held out his hand as Amon Carter said, "Will Rogers, I want to introduce you to President Calvin Coolidge." As Rogers shook his hand Rogers said, "I'm sorry, I didn't get the name." Coolidge broke out into a hearty laugh. Without a word, Carter opened his billfold and gave Rogers the $50.

Coolidge, incidentally, enjoyed having someone rub his forehead with petroleum jelly while he ate his breakfast in bed. When told that President Coolidge had died, Dorothy Parker said, "How could they tell?"

Will Rogers once remarked, "I don't belong to an organized political party. I am a Democrat."

In 1938 W. Lee "Pappy" O'Daniel of Texas was part of a radio program featuring a singing group, The Lightcrust Doughboys sponsored by Lightcrust Flour Company. When he off-handedly mentioned on the air that he might run for governor, he received 54,999 letters urging him to run. He ran and was elected after which wags said that six flags and a flour sack had flown over Texas.

When Warren Austin was the U.S. Ambassador to the United Nations, he earnestly suggested that the Jews and Arabs resolve their differences in a true Christian spirit.

Churchill ran in election against Labor Party's Clement Atlee. Scathing in his criticism of Atlee, a reporter said to Churchill,

"But at least you must admit that Atlee is humble." "He has a lot to be humble about," snorted Churchill.

Churchill also remarked about the French that it was impossible to govern a nation with 400 cheeses.

Isaiah Berlin worked for the British Information Service in World War II. His brilliant dispatches impressed Churchill who asked that he be invited to lunch. At the lunch the Prime Minister asked, "Berlin, what do you think is your most important piece that you've done lately?" His guest replied after hesitation, "White Christmas." It turned out that the invitation had mistakenly gone to **Irving** Berlin!

Once Churchill got a memorandum from Anthony Eden. He sent it back to Eden, writing across the margin, "This document seems to contain every cliche except 'God is love' and 'Please adjust your dress before leaving.'"

Another time George Bernard Shaw invited Churchill to the first night of one of his plays, enclosing two tickets "so that you can bring a friend, if you have one." Churchill, never at a loss for words, replied that unfortunately he couldn't come the first night but would be delighted to attend the second night, "if there is one."

At a party Lady Astor said to Churchill, "If I were your wife, I'd put poison in your coffee." "If you were my wife," he replied, "I would drink it!"

Churchill once said that the trouble with the Balkans is that the region produces more history than it can consume.

Я

I've always thought that if the French took control of the Rock of Gibraltar they should change its name to "DeGaulle Stone."

☞

After the Army-McCarthy hearings, someone commented that it was the first time since Samson that an army had been slain by the jawbone of an ass.

Я

Harry Golden remarked during the campaign of Senator Goldwater for the presidency, "I always knew that if America elected a Jew as president, he would be an Episcopalian."

☞

Goldwater's friends campaigned for him with the slogan, "In your heart you know he's right." "Far right," countered his frightened opponents. Others said, "In your guts you know he's nuts." At the tumultuous Democratic Convention in Chicago in 1968, Mayor Richard Daley stated that "the policeman isn't there to create disorder; the policeman is there to preserve disorder."

Я

I'll never forget when John Connally became a Republican right in the middle of the Watergate scandal. A reporter asked Texas' liberal, former Senator Ralph Yarborough for a comment. Yarborough replied, "It is the only time in history that a rat swam to a sinking ship."

In retrospect, the name of Nixon's Committee to Re-elect the President – CREEP – was strangely fitting for the Watergate era.

The tough Margaret Thatcher in Britain was called by some "Attila the Hen." Clive James once said that a speech by Margaret Thatcher sounded "like the Book of Revelation read over a railroad station public address system by a headmistress wearing calico sneakers."

During Hubert Humphrey's campaign for president, I saw him on TV trying to shake off the legacy of the Vietnam War. He overdid it when he said, "I'll tell you this, my fellow Americans. No sane person in this country likes this war. And neither does President Johnson."

The ever loquacious Humphrey was referred to by Jimmy Carter at the national Democratic Convention in 1980 as "Hubert Horatio Hornblower."

An interviewer asked John Kennedy what music he liked and he replied, "'Hail to the Chief' has a nice ring to it.'"

John Kenneth Galbraith referred to 1980s Reaganomics as "horse and sparrow" economics: the idea that if you just give enough oats to horses, some will be discharged on the roads for the sparrows.

When President Samuel Doe of Liberia visited the White House, Reagan introduced him as "Chairman Moe."

Meeting with the foreign minister of Lebanon, Reagan said, "You know, your nose looks just like Danny Thomases."

The illegal and zany antics of Oliver North during "Irangate" could be called, "Cuckoo, Iran and Ollie."

Looking at the prospect of a Dukakis/Bush race in 1988, Mark Russell commented, "There isn't enough caffeine in the world to keep us awake for that." And, in observing that Philadelphia politics had gone from Franklin and Madison to Rizzo and Goode, he said that obviously proves that Darwin was wrong. He also said that the real question about Reagan's role in the Iran arms affair was, "Do jelly beans cause amnesia?"

Texas' populist Jim Hightower says that getting progressives together is like loading frogs into a wheelbarrow. And he adds, "The people are revolting." In challenging corporate power he reminds us, "No building is too tall for a small dog to lift its leg on."

Texas Democrats squared off at Bush during the Democratic Convention. Jim Hightower remarked that George Bush was born on third base and thought he'd hit a triple. In her keynote address, Ann Richards (later elected governor) brought down the house with her "Poor George. He was born with a silver foot in his mouth."

Despite the cruelty of the Marcos dictatorship, Filipinos never lacked for humorous references to Ferdinand and his avaricious wife Imelda. She was, they said, head of the "Mink Dynasty." At the height of press censorship *The Manila Journal* was referred to as "the Manila urinal." Politically powerful Cardinal Sin finally turned against Marcos and led the call for the 'people power' revolt. After the revolt it was widely said that Marcos lost the revolution because he was "without Sin." It was also because he had the guns, Cory Aquino had the nuns. In fact they made it a nunviolent revolution.

In the Philippines election of 1992, the combative presidential candidate Miriam Defensor Santiago was called "the mouth that roared."

Then there is the old story of Sir Charles James Napier who captured Sind in India during the heyday of the British Empire. He is said to have telegraphed the British War Office the Latin word, "peccavi" ("I have sinned.")

Bob Dole, in a debate with Ted Kennedy, said, "I want to tax your memory." "Why didn't I think of that?" replied Kennedy.

Governor Frank Licht of Rhode Island, while campaigning for George McGovern for president in 1968, declared, "Nixon has been sitting in the White House while George McGovern has been exposing himself to the people of the United States."

President Lyndon Johnson asked Baptist Bill Moyers to open the cabinet session with prayer. As Moyers prayed, LBJ said, "Speak up, Bill. I can't hear you." "I wasn't speaking with you, Mr. President," replied the soft-spoken Moyers.

A.J. Liebling said, "Freedom of the press is guaranteed only to those who own one."

After Margaret Thatcher stepped down as Prime Minister (finally!), it is said that President Bush telephoned her to inquire what she thought of John Major, who was pretty much of an unknown quantity to Americans. "Oh, he's brilliant," she replied. "How do you know?" asked Bush. "Well, he passed my intelligence test in a flash." "What is that test?" asked Bush. "Well," she said, "I asked him 'Who is the son of your father who is not your brother?' 'It is I,' said Major immediately, proving his superior intelligence." The next day Bush asked Quayle, "Dan, who is the son of your father who is not your brother?" "I'll need some time to think about that," said Quayle. "Oh, all right" said Bush impatiently. That night Quayle called Kissinger and asked him, "Dr. Kissinger, who is the son of your father who is not your brother?" "It is I," said Kissinger immediately. The next day Quayle told Bush that he had the answer to the riddle": "It is Dr. Kissinger." "No, dummy," said Bush. "It is John Major!"

It was also said that Dan Quayle thought that Roe vs. Wade had to do with two ways to cross the Potomac River.

Jokes aside, the press developed a "gaffe watch" on Dan Quayle due to the large number of mistakes he made in his public utterances. One of the best known occurred when he was speaking for the United Negro College Fund, which has the motto, "A mind is a terrible thing to waste." Quayle said, "What a waste it is to lose one's mind, or not to have a mind, is being very wasteful. How true that is."

Another time, commenting on what was happening in the USSR during Gorbachev's policies of perestroika, Dan Quayle said, "Nothing has changed (in the USSR), and it could change back in a moment."

Once Quayle, speaking of the importance of bonding between parents and their children, said, "Republicans understand the importance of bondage between parent and child."

When the Clinton transition team cleared out Quayle's office, they found stationery with a letterhead that said:
Office of the Vice President, The Council on Competativeness

What chord was struck when a piano fell on the former prime minister of England? "A Flat Major."

During tough negotiating sessions preparing for the 1992 Earth Summit in Rio de Janeiro, Singapore's Tommy Koh was asked how he was sleeping. "Like a baby," he said. "I wake up every hour and cry myself to sleep again."

During the 1992 presidential primary in New Hampshire – a state mired in a deep recession – the First Lady was greeted with a sign that said, "We love you Barbara, but you are sleeping with the enemy."

Ross Perot during an interview said, "Revitalizing General Motors is like teaching an elephant to dance."

Johnny Carson remarked, "Unlike communists, democracy does not mean having just one ineffective political party; it means having two ineffective political parties."

My favorite political columnist today is Molly Ivins from Texas, who writes regularly for *The Texas Observer, The Progressive* and *The Fort Worth Star-Telegram*. Sassy, witty and astute, she has a populist passion for the underdog and scorn for the rich and powerful whose policies benefit the few and the mighty, whom she called, during the Bush years, the "Bushwazee."

She observes that "Texans shoot each other a lot. You can get five years for murder and ninety-nine for pot possession in this state." In her bestseller *Molly Ivins Can't Say That, Can She?*, she tells about an incident at Scholz Beer Garten in Austin when she, Ann Richards (former Governor of Texas), the State Comptroller Bob Bullock and Bullock's head of personnel – a black man named Charlie Miles – were talking at the back of the Garten. An East Texas judge, well known for his racist views, came up and greeted Bullock, "Bob, my boy, how are yew?" "Judge, I want you to meet my friends. This is Molly Ivins of *The Texas Observer*."

"How yew, little lady?" said the judge.

"This is Charles Miles who heads my personnel department." Charlie stuck out his hand and the judge got an expression on his face as though he had just stepped in a fresh cowpie. It took him a long minute before he reached out, barely touched Charlie's hand and said, "How yew, boy?" Then he turned with great relief to pretty blue-eyed Ann Richards and said, "And who is this lovely lady?"

"Ann beamed and said, 'I am Mrs. Miles.'"

After the interminable daily headlines in 1998 about Monica Lewinksy, the satirist Mark Russell asked what would it take to end the obsession with the White House scandal: "Saddam Hussein at Camp David? Or John Doe No. 5? Or how about at the Academy Awards Elia Kazan naming Charlton Heston as a communist?"

In a letter to the editor, someone from Sydney wrote, "Thank God Australia got the convicts and United States got the Puritans."

PEACE
MOVEMENT
HUMOR

PEACE MOVEMENT HUMOR

Will Rogers observed, 'You can't say civilization isn't advancing. In every war they kill you in a new way."

During the Vietnam war there was an anti-war protest in Kalamazoo, Michigan. As the police arrested the group committing civil disobedience, someone yelled, "You can't do that in the Soviet Union." Jack Payden-Travers called back, "You can't do it here either!"

Syndicated columnist Dave Barry defines the Monroe Doctrine as having three parts:
1) Other nations are not allowed to mess around with the internal affairs of nations in this hemisphere.
2) But we are.
3) Ha, ha, ha.

During an all-night peace vigil at the US Capitol during the Vietnam War, a priest came in the middle of the night to give bread and wine to the group. As he went from person to person, one woman said, "Sorry to decline, but I am Jewish." "Well," said the priest, "You don't have to be Christian for this. This is more a symbol of our solidarity together in the struggle for a peaceful world." "Well, all right," said the woman. As the priest handed her the bread he said, "This is the body of Christ." The woman pulled back, saying, "Oh, I am also vegetarian."

Probably the most successful, hilarious and truly antiwar series ever to run on television was M*A*S*H. As Patricia Helman wrote in *The Christian Century* (March 23-30, 1983), "Hawkeye's fans were laughing so hard that they hardly noticed the program's message: War goes to the center of hell. It is a madness perpetrated on the young and the powerless by powers and principalities out of touch with its reality and distanced from its white-hot center of brutality and suffering. It springs from a profane perception of the world and of human life." Countering this madness were the zany characters of the 4077th Mobile Army Surgical Hospital of whom Helman would say, "I celebrate M*A*S*H because under all the tomfoolery, the wit, the magnificent monotony of life in the Swamp, its characters are singing a sacred song. They are fair-minded, compassionate human beings, bitter to the bone at what they are called to do." Thus when Hawkeye is asked by a correspondent, "Do you see anything good at all coming out of this war?" he answers, "Yeah, me alive...That would be nice." Another time Hawkeye says, "I just don't know why {the Koreans} are shooting at us. All we want to do is bring them democracy and white bread, to transplant the American dream: freedom, achievement, hyperacidity, affluence, flatulence, technology, tension, the inalienable right to an early coronary at your desk while plotting to stab your boss in the back. That's entertainment." The series' original head writer, Larry Gilbert, called M*A*S*H "the Marx Brothers in 'All Quiet on the Western Front.'"

A peace group in Spring Valley, New York during the Gulf war called itself "the Kuwait Watchers." That was after Kuwait had been Saddamized. Many people were asking what the US would have done in response to Saddam if Kuwait's major export were broccoli instead of oil.

Gandhi said, "If I had no sense of humor I should long ago have committed suicide." This sense of humor was often seen in his writings, even on the most serious topics:

"God has given enough for everyone's need, but not enough for everyone's greed."

"An eye for an eye and a tooth for a tooth will leave the whole world blind and toothless."

When asked what he thought of Western civilization, Gandhi replied, "I think it would be a good idea."

Once Gandhi had tea with the King of England. The Mahatma wore his usual dress: a homespun loincloth. When later asked if he had felt under-dressed, Gandhi replied that the King had worn enough clothes for the two of them.

The newspaper *Ground Zero* had a regular column, "Letters to Gandhi," imaginary humorous correspondence between Gandhi and peace activists, such as:

Dear Gandhi:
For the past 100 days in jail, I've had this vast craving for pizza, with no way to fulfill the lust. Did you ever use pizza in your experiments with truth?

Bemused behind bars,
Thornton Kimes

(Kimes was serving a six-month jail sentence for cutting the fence at a missile silo in Conrad, Montana.)

Dear Thornton:

Yes, my experiments began with the recognition that we all have a pizza the truth.

Gandhi

It is said that Gandhi walked barefoot everywhere so that his feet were very hardened. A man of prayer, he often fasted so that he became thin and frail. In addition, due to his eating habits he developed bad breath. As a result he was known as a super calloused fragile mystic plagued with halitosis.

Two German spies dropped into England in World War II. They went into a bar and ordered martinis. "Dry?" asked the bartender. Holding up two fingers, one quickly answered, "Zwei."

Rainer Hildebrant tells of the East German who was arrested for distributing unsanctioned leaflets. He was taken to the police station whereupon the police discovered all the leaflets were blank pieces of paper. They demanded to know what he was up to. The protester said, "Anything I would write on a leaflet everyone already knows." The police therefore released him but he had made his point.

Daniel Berrigan—Jesuit priest, poet and prophet—has a keen sense of humor that is a delight. During the war in Vietnam, Dan was part of the action in which selective service files in Catonsville, Maryland were burned. Noting that many seemed to be more upset by burning files than by napalm-burned bodies in Vietnam, Dan decided to go underground rather than recognize the authority of the government in convicting him of a criminal act. Although he was widely sought by the FBI, for months he successfully remained in hiding, reappearing from time to time to preach or meet with various groups. Once at a big anti-war rally in Ithaca, New York, FBI agents were scattered around the auditorium as there was expectation that Berrigan would be there. The MC pointed to a door in the back of the stage and said that it was the door from which the prophet Elijah would appear. Sure enough, during the program out walked Berrigan whereupon the FBI agents sprang from the audience and started for the stage. By pre-arranged plans, the lights in the auditorium went out and Dan climbed into one of the large Bread and Puppet theater puppets resting on stage and when the lights came back on, he was gone.

Dan went to Block Island in Rhode Island for refuge. One day, during a terrible blowing storm, he looked out of his window and saw two FBI agents hiding the bushes, pretending to be bird hunters, wearing orange rain coats and looking through binoculars. They seized Dan, handcuffed him and took him by boat to the mainland. They got seasick in the roiling waters but not Dan. Pictures in the newspapers the next day showed him beaming as he is carted off to jail by the two grim agents.

Dan continued to protest the war, committing civil disobedience at various actions. At a trial in 1990 in Norristown, Pennsylvania, the judge asked him if he had been convicted of any other felonies since the Plowshares Eight action at King of Prussia in 1980. He wasn't sure and asked former Attorney General Ramsey Clark. Clark wasn't sure either. The prosecuting attorney told the judge that Berrigan had not and the judge accepted his opinion. Dan then spoke up, "But your honor, that doesn't mean that I don't have a criminal mind." The courtroom broke out in laughter and even the judge joined in.

Later in the proceedings, the judge said, "Father Berrigan, regardless of the outcome of these hearings, will you promise the court that you will refrain from such acts in the future?" Dan replied that he was being asked the wrong question. Taken aback, the judge said, "O.K., Father Berrigan, what do you think is the proper question?" "Well, your honor," said Dan, "it appears to me that you should ask President Bush if he'll stop making missiles; and, if he'll stop making them, then I'll stop banging on them and you and I can go fishing."

Berrigan was an adviser for the movie "Mission" which was filmed in Paraguay.

He also had a bit part in the movie, playing the role of a missionary. His only line in the movie is when he says, "No." In talking about his role, he remarked that it was sort of like what he does in the church--saying "No."

When we celebrated Dan's 75th birthday at the FOR headquarters in Nyack, we arranged a display of Berrigan memorabilia in a wooden display case in the lobby. When I pointed it out to him, he said, "It looks like my coffin." But my favorite birthday story about Dan occurred at the Pax Christi celebration of his 70th birthday in New York City. After dinner a huge cake with 70 burning candles was brought out and placed in front of him. The hundreds gathered became quiet, expecting him to blow out the candles. Instead, he simply sat there and watched all the candles as they one by one melted down and went out. We were all delighted, so to speak.

Billy Graham preached in Edinburgh, Scotland at the height of the Cold War when there were great fears about nuclear war. Lord George MacLeod, Moderator of the Church of Scotland and IFOR President, went up to Graham during a reception and said, "Billy, what do you think of nuclear weapons?" Replied Graham, "Well, I am an evangelist and my job is to lead people to Christ. Once they have been saved, then they will know how to deal with questions like that." "Well, Billy," said MacLeod, "you've been saved. What do you think of nuclear weapons?"

George MacLeod maintained his radical outlook even as a member of the House of Lords. Commenting on his speeches there he remarked, "I open my mouth and they close their ears. It's a perfect match."

Lily Tomlin observed that "no matter how cynical you get it's almost impossible to keep up." Which is why we heed Molly Ivins advice, "Have fun while fighting for freedom. For one thing, it may be the only fun you'll ever have."

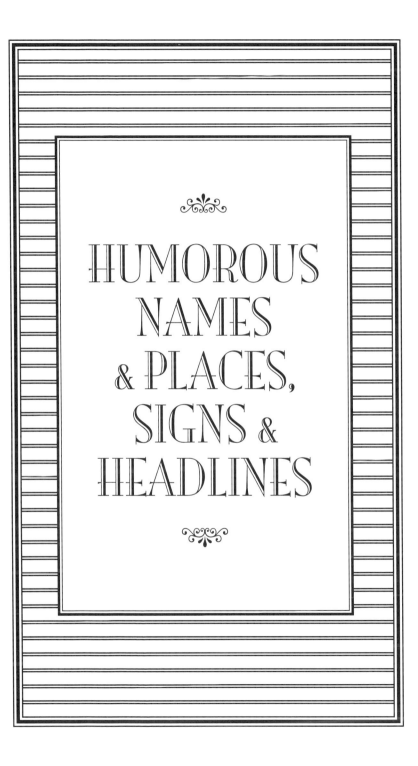

HUMOROUS NAMES & PLACES, SIGNS & HEADLINES

HUMOROUS NAMES
& PLACES, SIGNS
& HEADLINES

Flushing Friends Meeting (in Flushing, New York)

Slap Out Methodist Church (in Slap Out, Oklahoma)

Cannon Ball Church (in Cannon Ball, North Dakota)

Intercourse, Pennsylvania

Muleshoe, Texas

Bucksnort, Tennessee

Philpott Florists (in Abilene, Texas)

Sniffen Funeral Home (in Spring Valley, New York)

Frost Free Library (in Marlborough, New Hampshire)

Purdy Outhouse

Ginger Screws Casanova

Patti Breedlove (director of Planned Parenthood in Passaic County, New Jersey)

Ima Hogg (daughter of Gov. James Hogg of Texas) Contrary to popular belief she did not have a sister named Ura. Ima became a much loved philanthropist and founder of the Houston Symphony and the Hogg Mental Health Foundation. Born in 1881, Ima—a shortened form of Imogene—died in 1975.)

E. Pluribus Eubanks

Lobelia Rugtwit Hildebiddle

Fanny Hunnybun

Cardinal Sin

Father Sinner

Rev. Boozer

Rev. I. B. Loud

Pastor Dallas Darling

Rick Nutt

Bear Hollyday

Ruth Dreamdigger

Tashi Leo Lightning

Judy Formica

Robin Rockafellow

Comingwen D. Pond

B.M. Keese

B.A. Blessing

Eloda Maneure

Prude Ranch (a religious conference center)

The Crummy Chair of Evangelism

The Howfirma Foundation

Curl Up & Dye (beauty salon in Redondo Beach, California)

Endangered Feces (supplier of fossils in Tuscaloosa, Alabama)

Sacred Heart of Jesus Bingo

Holy Rood Church

The Little Shop of Horas (music shop in Cambridge, Massachusetts)

Foreign Wide (gift shop in New Paltz, New York)

Khant Gho Wong (Chinese restaurant in Charton, Massachusetts)

"Good Cod, what food these morsels be" (sign in seafood restaurant in Lincoln, Nebraska)

Payne & Lovett (dentists in Abilene, Texas)

Barber of C'ville (barber shop in Centerville, Massachusetts)

Just Desserts (bakery chain in California)

The Great Steak Out (restaurant in Great Barrington, Massachusetts)

Squid Row (seafood restaurant in Manhattan)

One Night Stand (clothing rental store)

Latter Day Shirts (cleaners in Salt Lake City)

Pizza, Paul and Mary (pizza place in Vermont)

Love & Quiches, Ltd. (in Freeport, New York)

Lubbock or Leave It (country store in Austin, Texas)

Dr. Shake (chiropractor)

Dr. Butcher (surgeon)

Sacred Grounds (the coffee shop next to the Episcopal Cathedral of Chicago)

A man named **Lawless** ran for the office of District Attorney on Cape Cod

Go Away! (travel agency)

Hackenyack (barber shop in Seattle)

In the Philippines, one finds:

Our Lady of Perpetual Help Pawn Shop

Jesus' Seat Covers

The Immaculate Conception Maternity Hospital

No T-Shirt Allowed (sign in provincial airport)

No Parking Both Sides

In Tunapuna, Trinidad:

"No naked lights while the engine is running"
(sign at service station)

"Fresh pluck & gutt chicken"
A houseboat advertisement in Kashmir:

"Sentry fitted, flesh system" (according to Rae Mason who saw the sign, it meant "sanitarily fitted, flush system")

Signs along the road:

"We Buy Old Orientals" (sign in rug store in Nyack, New York)

"Caution   Slow   Construction"

"Gas   Food"

"Have You Hugged Your 50l(c)3 Today?"

"If you are thinking of crossing this pasture, I hope you are able to run a hundred yards in 9.03, for the bull can do it in 9.04" (seen by Glenn Smiley in Maine)

Actual bumper stickers:

Honk if you love peace and quiet

The gene pool could use a little chlorine

Forget about world peace. Visualize your turn signal

I feel like I'm diagonally parked in a parallel universe

If ignorance is bliss, why aren't there more happy people?

My favorite T-Shirts

"Cleopatra: Queen of Denial"

"Visualize Whirled Peas"

"I Can't Even Think Straight" (seen at Gay Pride March)

I hope to see on a T-Shirt

"You shall know the Truth and the Truth shall make you odd" (Flannery O'Connor)

Headlines I enjoyed
(some received as anonymous e-mail messages)

Kids Make Nutritious Snacks

Chef Throws His Heart into Helping Feed Needy

Astronaut Takes Blame for Gas in Spacecraft

British Left Waffles on Falklands

Police Begin Campaign to Run Down Jaywalkers

Iraqi Head Seeks Arms

Include Your Child When Baking Cookies

Red Tape Holds Up New Bridge

New Study of Obesity Looks for Larger Test Group

Panda Mating Fails. Vet Takes Over

Clinton Wins on Budget But More Lies Ahead

Two Sisters Reunited After 18 Years at Checkout Counter

From stories in the *Jerusalem Post*
Police Investigation of Murder Reaches a Dead End

Peres made no bones of the grave difficulties along the road to peace

Non-delivery of ram's horns meant that Israel's shofar export industry had suffered a bad blow

Prison commissioner said he'd transferred some lice-ridden prisoners to Ramle where some of the most hard-bitten criminals are kept

Bed-wetting device story floods the manufacturer with calls

When I was a boy I loved to read the series of simple wooden signs advertising Burma-Shave. I best remember:

Within This Vale
Of Toil and Sin
Your Head Grows Bald
But Not Your Chin.

Drinking drivers
Nothing worse
They put the quart
Before the hearse

Don't stick your elbow
Out too far
It might go home
In another car

Her chariot race
At eighty per
They hauled away
What had Ben Hur

– Burma-Shave

Signs seen in public restrooms:

In Kidapawan in the Philippines: **"Flash toilet after moving your vowels"**

At Calcutta airport: **"Gentle Men"**

At Pendle Hill (Quaker Center in Pennsylvania) in the rest-room located next to the meeting room:
"Do not flush toilet during meeting for worship. This means thee."

Sign in a truck stop in Indiana: **Hungary Man's Breakfast**

On a movie marque: **"Adam and Eve" With a cast of l000s**

Santa Fe gas station notice: **"We will sell gasoline to any-one in a glass container"**

Cleaners in New Mexico: **38 Years on the Same Spot**

Los Angeles Dance Hall: **Good clean dancing every night but Sunday**

In a funeral parlor: **Ask about our layaway plan**

On a maternity room door: **Push, Push, Push**

In a vet's waiting room: **Be back in 5 minutes. Sit! Stay!**

At a loan company: **Ask about our plans for owning your home.**

On a convent wall: **Trespassers will be prosecuted to the**

full extent of the law. — Sisters of Mercy

In an office: **Will the person who took the stepladder yesterday please bring it back or further steps will be taken**

Sign at an English farm: **Horse manure 50p per pre-packed bag. 20p do it yourself**

On a church door: **This is the Gate of Heaven. Enter ye all by this door (This door is locked because of the draft. Use the side door)**

"Wanted. Man to take care of cow that does not smoke or drink"

In a cocktail lounge in Oslo: **Women are requested not to have children in the bar**

In a safari park: **ELEPHANTS. Please stay in your car**

Notice in door of health food store: **Closed due to illness**

In a London office: **Toilet out of order. Please use floor below**

A cheese shop in Nazareth, Pennsylvania was referred to by area humorists as **"Cheeses of Nazareth."**

In Jamaica:
"Pimps, Prostitutes, Peddlars and Hairbraiding Not Allowed" (beach sign in Montego Bay)

Big Mama's Jerk Centre

Dud's Rental Cars

Jesus Love Little Children's Variety Restaurant

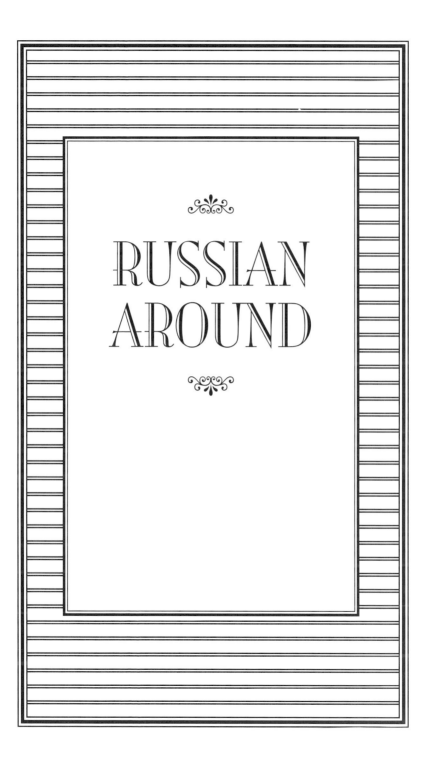

RUSSIAN
AROUND

RUSSIAN AROUND

❦ ❦ ❦ ❦ ❦ ❦ ❦ ❦ ❦ ❦ ❦

In my fourteen trips to what used to be the USSR – or what someone in early l99l called "the UFFR" (the Union of Fewer and Fewer Republics), and by late l99l pretty much fell apart – the very serious work of peacemaking and the teaching of nonviolence often found comic relief as I, and the various fellow travellers who accompanied me, had our funny bones tickled by laughing at sacred cows, word plays and just finding humorous incidents through endless miles on Aeroflot, Soviet trains, trams and subways. And best of all was the discovery that many ex-Soviets shared our sense of humor – especially as glasnost worked its way into the building of an open society.

But in the beginning it was rough, I must admit. In the pre-Gorbachevian days, they hadn't yet changed their Lenin and some things just weren't joking matters. On my first trip, in l982, I went on the Volga Peace Cruise. Some of my Vulga jokes were o.k. by Soviet standards – as when we docked at Volgagrad in front of the imposing stairs leading to a plaza and I asked, "Are those the steppes of Russia?" But I incurred the wrath of the Soviet passengers during a ship-board party we had. I was asked to M.C. the festivities, dressed as King Neptune. The conclusion of the many skits we planned was one in which an American tourist tells of getting arrested at Lenin's Tomb. "Why?" I asked, and was told that he had confused Lenin with John Lennon and was singing Beatles' tunes at the tomb. The Americans laughed; the Soviets glowered in anger. We had stepped on a sacred cow, there was no utter way to look at it. When we were back in Moscow, though, and the guide showed us the Kremlin wall in back of Lenin's tomb where the great communist heroes are buried, I told her, "Then this really is a communist plot." She laughed, so I made a few more cryptic remarks. I decided not to tell her another one that occurred to me:

when Lenin was dying, he called his closest aides around him and said, "Comrades, you will myth me," and he breathed his last. Very Intouristing.

Chris and Ralph Dull were on numerous FOR Journeys of Reconciliation and finally returned to live six months on a collective farm in Ukraine (compellingly recounted in their book, *Soviet Laughter, Soviet Tears*). They heard many of the jokes making the rounds in Ukraine as they worked and visited with the people. A few of my favorites they tell in their book:

A Russian is bragging. He says, "We have the world's biggest Metro, the world's biggest department store and the world's biggest computer chips."

One doctor says to the other, "Shall we treat the patient or let him live?"

"Why should we rejoice over the creation of a multiparty system?" asks a former Communist. "Just look what one party did to us!"

Q. Why don't Japanese and Soviets have AIDS?

A. Because AIDS is a disease of the 20th Century, and Japan is in the 21st Century and the USSR is in the 19th.

Perestroika is a lot of wind blowing the tops of the trees, but on the ground it's calm.

Perestroika for dogs: the chain is lengthened and barking is permitted, but the food dish is put farther away.

A collective farm sold 20 calves to the State and reported it to the District. The District reported to the Region that they sold 30.

The Region reported to the Republic that they sold 50.

The Republic reported to Moscow that they sold 100.

So Moscow decided to send 20 calves to Vietnam and keep the rest.

Latvia asked Moscow for independence for one year. The answer was no. Then they asked for independence for 2 weeks. The answer was still no. But when they asked Moscow for independence for 2 hours, Moscow said yes. So Latvia declared war on Sweden and surrendered to them five minutes later.

Gorbachev told this one on himself:

President Bush has 100 bodyguards and one of them is a terrorist, but he does not know which one.

President Mitterand has 100 lovers and one of them has AIDS, but he does not know which one.

And Gorbachev has 100 economic advisers. One of them is smart, but he does not know which one.

Before Gorbachev the common saying about the country's two leading newspapers, PRAVDA (which means "truth") and IZVESTIA (which means "news") was that PRAVDA is without izvestia and IZVESTIA is without pravda.

Two members of the Supreme Soviet were discussing the future of the country. "What we need," said one, "is a social democracy like Sweden's." "It is absolutely impossible" replied the other." "Why?" asked the first. "We don't have enough Swedes," he said.

The Russians sent up a space ship with 5 cows in it. It was the herd shot round the world.

In reporting the failed Soviet coup of August 19, 1991 Roger Simon reporting in *The Los Angeles Times* called it "the Koup Klutz Plan."

Before the fall of communism in Eastern Europe, there were plenty of jokes that poked fun at the system. Some of my favorites are:

How does the Polish Constitution differ from the American Constitution? Under the Polish Constitution citizens are guaranteed freedom of speech, but in the United States they are guaranteed freedom after speech.

How are the U.S. and Poland similar? In the United States you cannot buy anything for zlotys and in Poland you can't either. And in the U.S. you can get whatever you want for dollars, just as you can in Poland.

Poland's great openness was unusual in the Eastern bloc. This is demonstrated in this story: Two dogs meet in Warsaw's Old City. One is a Czech dog, well-fed and healthy looking. The other is an emaciated cur, from Poland. The Czech dog comes for a visit and tells the Polish dog that in Prague there is plenty to eat. "Then why have you come here?" asks the cur. "To bark," replies the Czech dog.

A Hungarian in Moscow wants to know the time. He sees a Russian approaching carrying two large suitcases. "What time is it?," he asks. The Russian puts down the suitcases and looks at his watch. "It is 1:15 and 12 seconds. The date is November 12, the moon is full and the atmospheric pressure is rising." The Hungarian is highly impressed and asks if the watch is Japanese. "No," replies the man. "This is a product of our own Soviet technology." "That is wonderful" says the Hungarian. "Yes," says the Soviet, straining to pick up the suitcases. "But these batteries are still a bit heavy."

Madeleine Albright, former US Delegate to the United Nations, whose father was Czechoslovak Ambassador to Yugoslavia from 1945 to 1948, used to introduce herself as "the daughter of the former ambassador from the former Czechoslovakia to the former Yugoslavia."

As post-communist societies tried to start over, the task proved extremely daunting, reminding East Europeans of the truth in the old adage, "It is easy to transform an aquarium into fish soup but it is much more complicated to reverse the process."

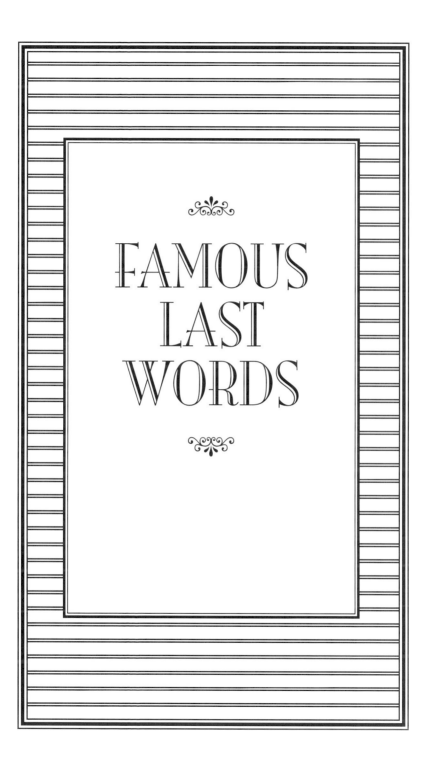

FAMOUS LAST WORDS

FAMOUS LAST WORDS

John Donne: "Would someone please go see whom they're ringing the bell for?"

Houdini: "I'll be right back."

Henry Kissinger: "Let me lie in state."

Finnegan: "Be sure to wake me."

Lenin: "You will myth me."

Ewell Gibbons: "That's a toadstool. This is a mush..."

Lot's wife: "No, no one is following us. Why do you ask?"

The Invisible Man: "Here goes nothing."

Ship Captain: "Don't give up the ship. Don't give up the blub...blub...blub."

Jean Sibelius: "Nice Finnish guys last."

Evel Knievel: "Oops."

General Custer: "Say, I hope I wasn't out of line with that crack about 'the only good Indian is a ......'"

The theater critic **Dorothy Parker** said that her own epitaph should be: "Pardon my dust."

When the beloved servant of the Clemens family died of burns after falling on the kitchen stove, **Mark Twain** was asked to write the epitaph. He thought a few moments and began chuckling, saying, "For the life of me, all I can think of is 'Well done, thou good and faithful servant.'"

RELIGIOUS HUMOR

RELIGIOUS HUMOR

A man falling off a cliff grabs a branch and as he hangs in mid-air, he looks heavenward and cries, "Is anyone up there?" An ethereal voice replies, "Let go and I will bear thee up." After a few moments, the man says, "Anyone else?"

A Zen disciple goes up to a hot-dog vendor in New York City's Central Park and says, "Make me one with everything."

A reception is held for a new Episcopal bishop in Washington, D.C. As the bishop is talking with a prominent Baptist minister, the waiter comes up and offers them a cocktail. The minister says, "I'd rather commit adultery than drink a cocktail." "Wouldn't we all?" smiles the bishop.

A swollen river brings a rising flood to a Louisiana valley. A National Guard jeep drives by an endangered house and the guardswoman tells the occupant to get in before the waters come. "God will take care of me," says the man. Soon the waters have flooded the first floor. A motorboat comes by and the man is offered a ride. "God will take care of me," says the man. Hours later the water has reached the roof. A helicopter flies by and the pilot tells the man, now on the roof, to climb in. "God will take care of me," he again replies. Soon the waters cover the roof and the man drowns. As he reaches heaven he complains to God for not saving him. "Look," says God. "I sent a jeep, a boat and a helicopter. What more do you expect?"

At the time of the scandals involving the TV evangelists, there were quite a few jokes that made the rounds. My favorites were these:

Jimmy Swaggart is writing a book entitled *Clergy Do More Than Lay People*.

Jerry Falwell's new book is *Repenthouse*.

And a movie about Jim and Tammy Bakker is entitled, "Children of a Looser God."

In a radio broadcast, a famous evangelist was referring to "a hale fellow, well met." But instead he said, "a hale wet male fellow." (a true story, by the way)

Once I received a letter asking if the Fellowship of Reconciliation was a non-prophet organization.

Church Bulletin Bloopers:

• The pastor will preach his farewell sermon after which the choir will sing, "Break Forth into Joy."

• Due to the rector's illness, the healing service on Wednesdays will be discontinued until further notice.

• Remember to pray for the many who are sick of our church and community.

• The 8th graders will be presenting Shakespeare's Hamlet in the church basement Friday at 7 pm. All are invited to attend this tragedy

- Low self-esteem support group will meet Thursday at 8 pm. Please use the back door.

- The audience is asked to remain seated until the end of the recession.

- The Ladies Bible Study will be held Thursday at 10 pm. All ladies are invited to lunch in the Fellowship Hall after the BS is done.

- Weight Watchers will meet at 7 pm. Please use the large double door at the side entrance.

When I went to Nicaragua with Witness for Peace, I heard many stories and jokes from Catholics about Pope John Paul. My favorites are these two: "What is the difference between the pope and the usual tourist who comes to Nicaragua?" "The tourist walks on the ground and kisses the women. The pope kisses the ground and walks on the women." Then there is the one about the pope being told by God that God will directly answer any questions he asks. The pope meditates a while, then says, "Oh God, will there be married priests?" "Not in your lifetime," assures God. The pope meditates a while longer, then says, "Lord, will there be women priests?" "Not in your lifetime," says God. Finally the pope says, "Oh God, will there be another Polish pope?" "Not in My lifetime," says God.

My friend, Jerry Anderson, once preached a particularly stirring sermon after which a parishioner shook his hand, exclaiming, "Oh, Rev. Anderson, if I never hear you again I'll be satisfied."

Children love the story of the girl who, after taking her teddy bear to church, decided to name it "Gladly." Her Sunday school teacher asked why and the girl said, "Because it is cross-eyed." "I don't understand" said the teacher. "You know," said the girl, "in church we sing about 'Gladly, the cross I'd bare'."

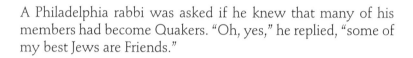

A Philadelphia rabbi was asked if he knew that many of his members had become Quakers. "Oh, yes," he replied, "some of my best Jews are Friends."

One of Naomi Goodman's young nieces had just moved into a new neighborhood. The little boy next door told her he was Catholic and asked what she was. "I'm not sure," she replied," but I think we're jewelry."

The theologian Paul Schilling told me the true story of a seminary president who, in welcoming a visiting chapel preacher, finished his lavish introduction by saying, "Our guest will speak out of his heart and out of his mind."

At the Chevy Chase Presbyterian Church, the minister started the children's sermon by asking, "What is salt used for?" After a few moments, one of the boys said, "Killing slugs."

A friend of mine was in a prayer group where one of the members began his prayer, "O Lord, forgive us for our falling shorts."

A woman told Thomas Carlyle that she had decided to accept the universe. "Egad," Carlyle responded, "you'd better."

G. K. Chesterton said, "The reason angels fly is that they take themselves so lightly."

H. L. Menken defined Puritanism as "the lurking fear that somewhere someone may be having a good time."

An Eastern sage, recounting how the world was created, told a group of seekers the legend that the earth is supported by resting on the back of a turtle. "Then what supports the turtle?" "It sits on the back of another turtle." "And what about the other turtle?" persisted the questioner. The sage was greatly irritated as he exclaimed, "Don't keep asking foolish questions. It's turtles all the way!" (also from Paul Schilling)

When told that Oscar Levant had converted from Judaism to Christian Science, Milton Berle is alleged to have said, "Our loss is their loss."

Glenn Smiley tells of the minister who visited an elderly parishioner and asked her if she ever thought about the hereafter. "All the time," she said. " I go into the kitchen and wonder, 'Now what did I come in here after?'"

Harry Emerson Fosdick, famous minister of New York City's Riverside Church, wrote in his autobiography about bringing his granddaughter and her little friend with him to his church, which is right across Riverside Drive from Grant's Tomb. He overheard his granddaughter tell her friend, "This is Gramp's tomb and that is Gramp's church."

Did you hear about the Unitarian who married a Jehovah's Witness? Their children still knock on people's doors, but they don't know why.

An Anglican clergyman, departing for England after giving a series of lectures in Scotland, was asked how he liked Scotland. "The country has its good qualities," he said, "but it has three serious drawbacks. It's always raining. It's too cold. And there are too many Presbyterians." "In that case," replied his host, "I suggest you go to hell. It never rains. It's always hot. And there are no Presbyterians."

Woody Allen gave a commencement address in which he told the graduates, "More than any other time in history, humanity faces a crossroads. One path leads to despair and utter hopelessness. The other, to total extinction. Let us pray we have the wisdom to choose correctly."

After taking their vows, the couple in a wedding ceremony knelt on the kneeling bench in front of the altar. Unknown to the groom, someone had written on the bottom of his shoes, "H E L P !"

Examples of Buddhist humor:

First the bad news: There is no key to unlock the mysteries of the universe.
Now the good news: The door has been left unlocked.

In a monastery where the inhabitants have taken a vow of silence, the monks are allowed to speak once every five years.

"What would you like to say this year?" asks the head monk.

"Well," says the monk, "it would be nice if the soup were served a little warmer."

"Thank you," replies the head monk.

Another five years go by. "What would you like to say this year?" asks the head monk.

"Well," says the monk, "our meditation cushions are getting lumpy and really need to be replaced."

"Thank you," says the head monk.

Another five years pass, and he asks, "What would you like to say this time?:

"Well," says the monk, "don't you think it's about time we allowed women into the order?"

"I don't know why you stay here," says the head monk. "All you've been doing for the last fifteen years is complaining, complaining, complaining."

(from the newsletter of the Buddhist Peace Fellowship)

Sign in a peace office: "I am a Quaker. In case of emergency, please be quiet."

The Rev. Henry Ward Beecher once received a letter with the single word, "Fool!" He told his congregation, "I have known many an instance of a man writing a letter and forgetting to sign his name, but this is the only instance I have ever known of a man signing his name and forgetting to write the letter."

❀

Archbishop Michael Peers, primate of the Anglican Church of Canada, received a letter requesting information from the Wisconsin Regional Primate Research Center for an "International Directory of Primatology." The archbishop's secretary wrote in response: "I think the primates in your study are perhaps a different species. While it is true that our primate occasionally enjoys bananas, I have never seen him walk with his knuckles on the ground or scratch himself publicly under the armpits."

✦

Was it W. H. Auden who said, "Christians are put in this world to help others. What the others are here for I haven't the slightest idea"?

❀

Mark Twain once remarked, "The rain is famous for falling on the just and unjust alike, but if I had the management of such affairs, I would rain softly and sweetly on the just, but if I caught a sample of the unjust outdoors, I would drown him."

✦

At a Hebrew school in New York City the teacher said, "The Lord our God is one." "When will He be two?" asked one of the children.

❀

When I was working in the Philippines, Methodist Bishop Jose Valencia retired. A printed program that honored the bishop said that he had been presented with "a number of plagues" by various church groups.

✳

In Hong Kong there was a schism in The True Jesus Church. The new congregation called itself The True, True Jesus Church.

✳

Dr. John Dickhout and Dr. Walter Dickhout were ministers of note, one being a seminary president, the other being a United Methodist district superintendent. At an event recognizing the outstanding ministries of the two men, the moderator announced to the congregation, "The two Dicksout will be happy to greet you at the door."

✳

A well-known Anglican clergyman crossing the Atlantic was asked by the steward how he should be addressed. "You can call me professor, mister, doctor, canon or father." "Thank you very much, reverend," the steward replied.

✳

Incidentally, the three types of Anglicans are: high and crazy, low and lazy, broad and hazy. Texan Melinda Moore calls Episcopalians "Catholic Light. All the ritual, half the guilt." And she says Methodists think you have to have a covered dish to get into heaven. Another Texan saying is that Baptists and cats are the only things in the world that can fight and multiply at the same time.

✳

A Methodist minister held a funeral for a member who had been a veteran. At the cemetery an honor guard shot its rifles according to military custom. As the shots rang out, the widow sighed and collapsed on the ground. Her little grandson screamed, "Those bastards shot grandma!"

Sign in front of a church (in a John Callahan cartoon):
"Beware of Dogma"

Easter sermon topic seen on the sign of a Unitarian church in Boston: "You Can't Keep a Good Man Down."

In commenting on conflicts between oppressors and the oppressed, Archbishop Tutu says, "When the elephant has its foot on the tail of a mouse and you say you are neutral, the mouse will not appreciate your neutrality."

Nancy Forest told me the Jewish story of the man who says to the Lord, "Is it true that in your scale of reckoning a thousand years is like a minute?" The Lord assures him that it is. "And is it true that in your weights and measures, a thousand dollars is like a penny?" Again the Lord assures him that that is right. The man then says, "Lord I am a poor man. Give me a penny." The Lord says, "In a minute."

A Salvation Army group was giving its testimony on a street corner. The man playing the bass drum was asked to speak. "Well," he began, "before I was converted, I led a wild life. I drank all the time, I caroused on the weekends, I gambled away every paycheck. But since I've been converted," he said and then paused for a moment, "all I do is beat this damn drum."

An elderly, childless couple often spoke of how much they loved children. One day, they had a new sidewalk put down at the front of their property. Before the cement dried, some neighborhood children ran across it. When the husband discovered what had happened, the footprints had already hardened in the concrete. He went in the house yelling how much he hated kids and that he would never forgive them. "But, dear," said his wife, "you've always loved children. How can you say such a thing?" "Well," he grumbled, "I guess I love them in the abstract, but not in the concrete!"

Archbishop Tutu was walking past a construction site in Capetown. There was a temporary sidewalk only wide enough for one person to walk on it at a time. A white man at the other end of the sidewalk recognized the archbishop and said, "I don't give way to gorillas." Upon which Tutu stepped aside, made a low sweeping gesture and said, "Ah, yes, but I do."

At a Presbyterian service of ordination, several ministers lay their hands on the head of the young minister being ordained. "What are they doing?" a puzzled girl in the congregation asks her father. "They're removing his spine," the father replied.

A pastor knocked repeatedly on a parishioner's door. Although he clearly heard the TV on inside, no one came to the door. As he left he pushed his calling card under the door, writing on the back, "Revelation 3:20. Behold, I stand at the door and knock. If anyone will open, I will come in." The next Sunday a woman at church handed him a card that read, "Genesis 3:10. I heard thy voice and was naked, so I hid myself."

A Sufi saying: Never try to teach a pig to sing. It only frustrates the teacher and irritates the pig.

Matthias Neuman, OSB, reminds us that "Jewish spirituality always found a place for humor. It has not forgotten that the biblical God is a God of unexpected turns, twists, and surprises. God plays; God teases! Jewish spirituality loves the humor of a laughing insight into religion. Even the classics – the Talmud, the Zohar, the Hasidic stories – revel in the humorous tidbit: 'If one man calls you an ass, ignore it. If two or three call you an ass, start looking for a saddle.'"(from an article in *America*, quoted in *The Joyful Noiseletter, Epistle of the Fellowship of Merry Christians*, October 1991) And the comedian Joe E. Brown, who was popular when I was a boy, said: "I could not be interested in any man's religion if his knowledge of God did not bring him more joy, did not brighten his life, did not make him want to carry this joy into every dark corner of the world. I have no understanding of a long-faced Christian. If God is anything, He must be joy!" (from Rev. John Walker of Post, Texas, quoted in *The Joyful Noiseletter*, October 1991)

My good friend, Mariquita Platov of the Orthodox Peace Fellowship, reminds us of the old tradition in the Russian Orthodox Church of holy fools, "fools for Christ" who traditionally were healers and peacemakers who spoke truth to power. That tradition is reviving today under the new freedoms in Russia.

In one of Mariquita's playlets she tells the story of Nicholas

Salos, a holy fool who lived in Pskov during the time of Ivan the Terrible. Once the cruel Czar came to Pskov with his army, intent on a massacre. Nicholas appeared on a child's hobby-horse crying out, "Ivanushka, Ivanushka, eat some bread and salt instead of human blood!" He invited the Czar to tea in Nicholas' cell in the bell tower of the church. He proceeded to serve the Czar a huge piece of raw meat. Ivan protested that he didn't eat meat during Lent. Nicholas told him that he did much worse, "feeding on human blood." Nicholas warned Ivan that he would be struck by lightning if a single child in Pskov was harmed. At that moment a servant ran in with the news that the Czar's horse had suddenly dropped dead. Ivan the Terrible fled from Pskov in terror.

The holy fools – just like the religious clowns springing up in many places – remind us to find a place in our religious communities for the unconventional and eccentric who speak the truth. Remember Flannery O'Connor's observation, "You shall know the truth and the truth shall make you odd."

Thomas Paul Thigpen writes in *The Joyful Noiseletter* (April 1991), "A Christian hymn dating from about the year 120 A.D. tells of Jesus' dancing with disciples at the Last Supper. Dance was used in the earliest recorded Christian liturgies. Justin Martyr (150 A.D.) and Hippolytus (200 A.D.) both describe joyful circle dances in the sanctuary. The church historian Eusebius wrote in the fourth century a detailed account of the dancing in one worship service, both spontaneous and choreographed. Clement of Alexandria, Gregory of Nyssa, John Chrysostom, Basil, Ambrose, Augustine and others wrote approvingly of praise dancing." That is a far cry from the funereal quality of many contemporary worship services.

G.K. Chesterton observed, "Life is serious all the time but living cannot be. You may have all the solemnity you wish in your neckties, but in anything important (such as sex, death and religion), you must have mirth or you will have madness."

In a similar vein, Garrison Keillor tells of Moses coming down from Mt. Sinai and telling the people, "I got him down to ten commandments. Unfortunately, adultery is still in but solemnity is out." Afterwards, the Israelites killed the fatted calf, drank wine and told Bible stories all night.

If you make a Unitarian mad, he'll burn a question mark in your lawn.

After my father died, my mother remarried a few years later. After her second husband died, she married for a third time. When she was 90 her third husband died. Then she died at the age of 92. As my wife and I prepared to go to the funeral, we gathered the grandchildren together for a prayer. When the prayer was over, 8 year old Christina said, "I'll bet Grandmother Helen is in heaven having fun with all her husbands."

A priest comes out to say the mass. He speaks into the microphone, "There's something wrong with this mike." "And also with you" replies the congregation

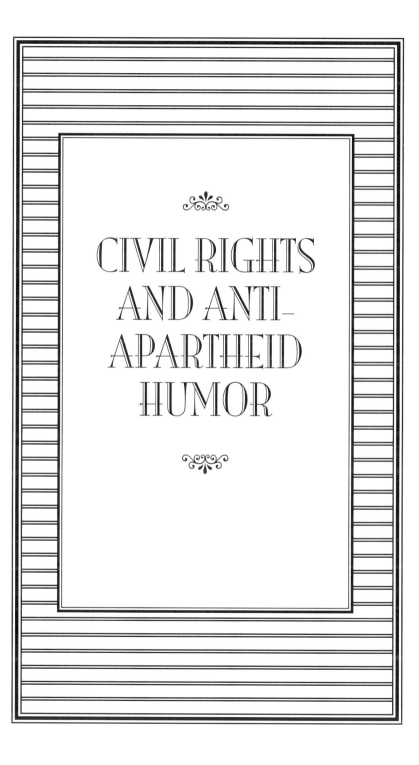

CIVIL RIGHTS AND ANTI-APARTHEID HUMOR

CIVIL RIGHTS AND ANTI-APARTHEID HUMOR

Great bursts of humor and laughter often characterized the struggle for civil rights. Even in situations of suffering and ominous danger, those working for justice found ways to pierce the gloom and restore hope with humor. Coretta King told me that many seem to have a mistaken opinion of Martin as a solemn, even humorless man, but she said they couldn't be more wrong. This is borne out by all those who worked with him.

Andy Young tells many funny stories about Martin Luther King and the SCLC staff who joked and roughhoused to let off steam. King loved to tell about the man who responded to his call for nonviolence by saying, "Aw right, Reverend, if you says so, but ah still think we oughta kill off a few of 'em."

Once, in an elevator in New York City, a white woman got on and said to Dr. King, "Six, please." Even though he had on a business suit and tie, she assumed he was the elevator operator. King pushed the "6" button. When the woman got off at the sixth floor, he burst out laughing after the door closed.

Wyatt Walker tells the story of a big Negro who was insulted by a white bus driver. He looked down at the driver and said, "I want you to know two things. One, I ain't no boy. And two, I ain't one of those Martin Luther King nonviolent Negroes."

In *Stride Toward Freedom*, King saw the humor in the white matrons who had no intention of being without their maids during the bus boycott and who therefore picked them up and took them home everyday. One of the matrons remarked to her maid, "Isn't this boycott terrible?" "Oh, yes ma'am," replied the maid. "it sure is. I just told all my young 'uns to stay off the buses till they get this thing settled."

FOR's Glenn Smiley, who worked with King during the boycott, liked the story of the Negro's dog that bit one of the white men opposing the boycott. The dog then went over to a Negro and bit him. "Now why did he do that?" someone asked. "Oh," said the owner, "I don't know—unless he just wanted to get that awful taste out of his mouth!"

Even in the most frightening moments of the struggle, the humor was there. After the three civil rights workers were killed near Philadelphia, Mississippi, SCLC called for a march and rally. When they gathered in Philadelphia, they saw hostile whites nearby. "Within the sound of my voice," said Dr. King, "there are those who know what happened to Goodman, Cheyney and Schwerner." From the back of the crowd, someone said, "You damned right!" At the end of the rally, King called on Ralph Abernathy to pray. The next day someone asked King why he had called on Abernathy to pray rather than praying himself. "In that crowd," joked King, "I wasn't about to close my eyes!"

One of the riddles of the time was, "What has four eyes and can't see?"

The answer: **Mississippi**

In the Albany campaign of l962, the new militance was given a humorous twist as the marchers sang,

"I'm comin', I'm comin'
And my head ain't bendin' low
I'm walkin' tall, I'm talking strong,
I'm America's NEW Black Joe."

On one campus signs mysteriously appeared on the trees. On one tree, the sign said, "This tree for white dogs only." On another, "This tree for black dogs only."

Harry Golden's newspaper, *The Carolina Israelite,* loved to lampoon segregation with such things as "The Stand-up Negro Plan." Since the problem in the South seemed to be when Negroes sat down, he proposed that all the chairs and benches be removed from churches, schools, restaurants and soda fountains. With everyone thereby standing, segregation would be ipso facto eliminated.

The "Out of Order" plan dealt with the signs on "Whites Only" and "Colored Only" facilities such as drinking fountains, waiting rooms and rest rooms. Golden proposed placing "Out of Order" signs over the "Whites Only" signs so that the white customers would use the "Colored Only" facilities when they were thirsty enough, tired enough, or had to go to the rest room urgently enough.

Once Golden wanted to see how well integration was proceeding in Alabama. He went to a hospital where there was a nurses' station serving both the "white" and "colored" wings of the

hospital. He surveyed the thermometers that were in three containers on a shelf. One said, "White, Oral." The second said, "Colored, Oral." The third simply said, "Rectal." Golden gave this story the title, "Gradual Integration."

A Ku Klux Klan rally was held at the state capitol in Austin, Texas. They were met by 5,000 Texans who turned and dropped their pants in a planned "Moon the Klan" counter rally!

The comedian Dick Gregory named his autobiography, "Nigger." In the book's dedication to his mother, Gregory says "Momma, just know that every time you hear that awful word they are advertising my book!"

When he was asked to take out a lifetime membership in the NAACP, he refused, saying he would just pay one week at a time—what if he woke up some morning with lifetime membership and found out the country had been integrated?

Gregory tells of being in the South and going into a restaurant to eat. The white waitress tells him "We don't serve Negroes here." "That's all right," he says, "I don't eat Negroes," and orders a whole chicken. When the waitress eventually brings him his meal, three white guys—Ku, Klux, and Klan come up behind him and say, "Boy, whatever you do to that chicken we are going to do to you." "So" says Gregory, "I picked up that chicken and I kissed it!"

At the great March on Washington in 1963, Gregory looked

out on the massive gathering of 250,000 persons. He quipped, "The last time I saw this many of us, Bull Connor was doing all the talking."

I heard Dick Gregory speak when the war in Vietnam ended. He had begun fasting until the war was over and and when it finally ended, he looked like a concentration camp victim. After his speech, someone asked, "Dick, if there is another war are you going to fast.?" "No way," he said. "If there is another war, I'm going to McDonald's and I'm going to eat until that war is over!"

Gregory credits his positive outlook on life to his mother who, he said, "always had a big smile, even when her legs and feet swelled from high blood pressure and she collapsed across the table with sugar diabetes. You have to smile twenty-four hours a day, Momma would say. If you walk through life showing the aggravation you've gone through, people will feel sorry for you, and they'll never respect you. She taught us that man has two ways out in life—laughing or crying. There's more hope in laughing." *(p. 25)*

SOUTH AFRICA'S ANTI-APARTHEID HUMOR

Like their brothers and sisters in the American South, the anti-apartheid movement had many humorous moments in the midst of tragedy. In 1989 at the height of the Defiance Campaign, police sprayed purple dye on the marchers in Cape Town. Out of that incident came a slogan of the movement, "The purple shall govern."

During his speech at a subsequent peace march in Cape Town on September 13, 1989, Archbishop Desmond Tutu said, referring to President F.W. De Klerk, "Mr. De Klerk, come and look at technicolour. They tried to make us one colour, purple, but we are the rainbow people, the people of a new South Africa." The Center for Intergroup Studies in Cape Town published a wonderful book of tactics used by the anti-apartheid movement. The book's title is **The Purple Shall Govern.**

The End Conscription Campaign, in opposing the call-up of thousands of South Africans for military service, decided to build a sandcastle on the beach symbolizing CapeTown's "Castle." About forty persons wearing "Stop the Call-up" T-shirts came to the beach and started erecting the sandcastle. They were soon approached by a constable and told they did not have a permit to build the sandcastle. Invoking state of emergency regulations, the police came gave the group ten minutes to take off their T-shirts, knock down the castle and leave!

Hilarious letters to the editor of the local newspaper followed the event. Two of the letter writers said:

"By now everybody knows that sandcastles can be subversive. I personally have stopped building them, because I have an innate aversion to breaking the law. I also discourage children from building them on our local beach, explaining to them that they are the innocent and unwitting tools of lawlessness and disorder."

"Let adults build sandcastles, and soon they would want to build the real thing, thus undermining the state. Fortunately this danger was recognised in time on Sunday, by both a small section of the public and the forces of law and order."

In another protest, people were told to protest apartheid by burning a candle in their front window. Police began trying to force people to put out their candles but could not keep up with the lights appearing everywhere. Once again the absurdity of apartheid policies was highlighted by the ludicrous spectacle of police rushing from house to house putting out candles.

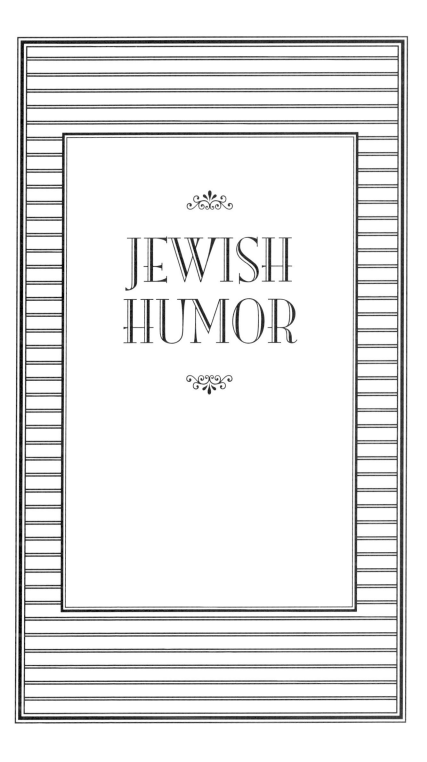

JEWISH HUMOR

JEWISH HUMOR

As Stefan Merken says, "History has dealt a funny card to the Jews." Out of exile and persecution has come, among many accomplishments, a rich sense of humor. A few examples:

A British Jew is waiting in line to be knighted by the Queen. He is instructed that the procedure is as follows: he is to kneel in front of the Queen and recite a sentence in Latin when she taps him on the shoulder with a sword. However, when his turn comes he is so excited that he forgets the Latin. Then, thinking fast, he recites the only other sentence he knows in a foreign language, which he remembers from the Passover seder: "Ma nishtana ha layla ha zeh mi kol ha laylot."

Puzzled, Her Majesty turns to her advisor and whispers, "Why is this knight different from all other knights?"

A journalist goes to Jerusalem and everytime she visits the Wailing Wall she sees the same old man praying at the wall. Finally she asks him, "I have seen you praying at the Wall every time I come here. How long have you been doing this?"

The bearded old man replies that he has been coming every day for 25 years. "In the morning I pray for world peace. I come back later and pray for the eradication of illness from the earth."

Amazed the journalist asks, "And how does it feel to do this sacred act daily for 25 years?"

The old man replies, "It feels like I'm praying to a wall."

Naomi Goodman's grandmother left two pounds of butter on the kitchen table, while she was occupied elsewhere. When she returned to the kitchen, the kitten was sitting on the table, next to the empty butter dish, licking its paws. Not one to jump to conclusions, she picked up the kitten and set it on the kitchen scale where it weighed exactly two pounds. In her perplexity, she asked: "If this is the butter, where is my kitten?"

Percy Goodman was fond of this story: Two brothers who were beggars used to visit a certain Baron de Rothschild once a year, around the time of the High Holy Days, at which time he would give each a valuable gold coin. This went on for a number of years. One year, the younger brother came alone. The Baron asked after his brother and was told he had died during the year. After the appropriate condolences, the Baron took out a single gold coin to give the survivor. The surviving brother rejected the coin, indignantly asking, "Who is my brother's heir? I or the Baron de Rothschild?"

Goodman also liked the story of the beggar in Vienna who stood outside Sacher's Restaurant to inhale the smells of the delicious food. The proprietors tried to drive him away, as they felt that it was bad for business to have this shabby beggar standing in front of the restaurant. But as he would not leave, they took him to court. The judge heard the case with great interest and agreed that the beggar should be fined, but, under the circumstances, the fine should be paid with the clink of a gold coin.

Upon leaving her native Lithuania in the 1920s, Freda Rosenblatt went to South Africa where she began acting in the Yiddish theater. In one play she had the leading role, that of a young woman who had fallen on hard times. At the end of the play she was to take poison and die. The final scene was never rehearsed as the rest of the cast never stayed around till the end. On the opening night Freda performed quite well. The coach, sitting in the wings, applauded her after each act. When the end came, Freda with great melodrama took the poison and staggered around the stage, grasping her throat, falling on the couch, rising dramatically and falling again. Unable to take it any longer the coach shouted, "Die already!" Freda could not contain herself: she broke out into laughter as did the audience as the curtain came down.

A rabbi gets carried away at the Yom Kippur service, prostrates himself on the floor and says, "Before you Lord, I am nothing." The cantor falls down next to him and cries out, "Before you Lord, I am nothing." In a few minutes Mr. Schwartz comes down and joins them, saying "Before you Lord, I am nothing." The rabbi looks at the cantor and says, "Look who thinks he's nothing."

Stefan Merken tells the story of Mrs. Goldberg who has two chickens. One is ill so she kills the healthy one and makes chicken soup to feed the sick one.

Centuries ago the pope decided that all the Jews had to leave Rome. Facing great resistance from the Jewish community the pope made a deal: he would have a debate with someone from the Jewish community. If the Jew won, the Jews could stay. If the pope won, the Jews would leave. The Jews realized they had no choice but to accept. No one, however, volunteered for the debate. Finally an old sweeper named Moishe agreed to debate the pope. He asked, however, that the debate be carried out in silence. The pope agreed to the condition.

The day of the great debate came. Moishe and the pope sat opposite each other in silence before the debate.Finally, the pope raised his hand and held up three fingers. Moishe looked back at him and raised one finger. The pope waved his fingers in a circle around his head. Moishe pointed to the ground where he sat. The pope pulled out a wafer and a glass of wine. Moishe pulled out an apple.

The pope stood up and said, "I give up. This man is brilliant. The Jews can stay." The cardinals gathered around the pope and asked him to explain his decision. The pope said, "First I held up three fingers to represent the Trinity. The old man responded by holding up one finger to remind me that there was still one God common to both our religions. Then I waved my finger around me to show him that God is all around us. He responded by pointing to the ground, showing that God is also right here with us. I pulled out the wine and the water to show that God absolves us from our sins. He pulled out an apple to remind me of original sin. He had an answer for everything. What could I do?"

Meanwhile, the Jewish community had crowded around Moishe, amazed that this poor, old man had done what all their great scholars had refused to attempt. "What happened?" they asked. "Well," said Moishe, "first he said to me that the Jews had three days to get out of here. I told him that not one of us was leaving. Then he told me that this whole city would be cleared of Jews. I let him know that we were staying right here." "And then?" asked a woman. "I don't know," said Moishe. "He took out his lunch and I took out mine."

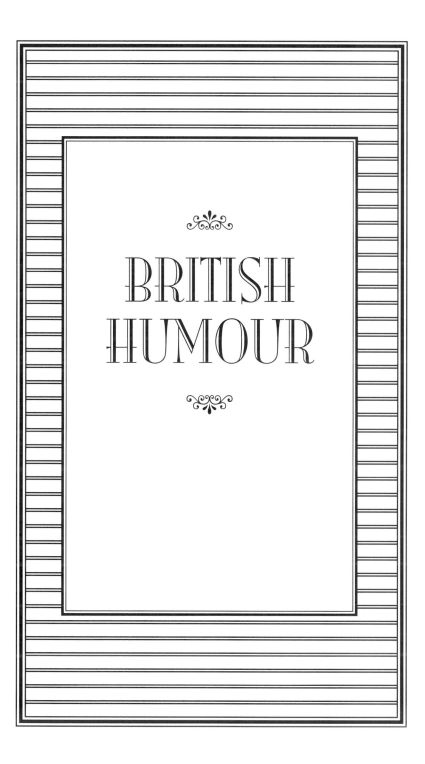

BRITISH HUMOUR

BRITISH HUMOUR

To some Americans, British humor is not very funny. But for others—myself included—it can be amusing, and often hilarious, even though the British sense of what is funny is at times quite different from what we in the US laugh at. Here are a few samples:

Two Englishmen meet. One says, "Terribly sorry to hear you buried your wife last week." "Had to," says the other one, "dead you know."

Diana Francis (past president of the International FOR) and her husband Nico, who live in Bath, have faxed me quite a number of jokes. One is about the brilliant young solicitor who was struck down dead. When he arrived at the gate of heaven he was extremely angry and berated St. Peter. "I am only 32 years old, I'm fit, never been ill in my life. You've made a serious mistake!"

St. Peter tried to calm him down and explained they never made mistakes. The young man continued to expostulate. He insisted that St. Peter check the files.

After a considerable delay, St. Peter returned with a cynical smile on his face. "Yes," he said, "there does seem to have been a mistake, but I think it is not ours but yours. You see, we added up the hours on your time-charge sheets to your clients, and it came to 87 years!"

The Francises also sent me some very funny stories from the British writer Adam Curle. One concerns the fellow named Hebblethwaite who met a man on a cold winter day who, as was his custom, had on only a light tweed jacket. "My dear fellow," said Hebblethwaite, who was wrapped up in a heavy overcoat, "you never wear an overcoat." The hearty fellow, laughing merrily, responded with pseudo-witticism, "No, I never was." *(Americans need to know that 'wear' and 'were' sound the same if you have a very upper-class English accent.)*

Mr. H thought this response was so marvelously funny that he rushed home, discarded all his outer coverings and immediately went out again into the cold, hoping that someone would ask him the same question. Nobody did.

Throughout the winter he shivered in only a light jacket. Many commented on his lack of suitable attire in such terms as 'Aren't you cold?' or 'You should wear an overcoat,' but no one expressed concern in such a way that he could make this wonderful joke.

At length he got a cold; it developed into flu and then pneumonia and, finally, double pneumonia. But the gallant fellow persisted in his quest for merriment. Finally, one day he collapsed. An ambulance took him, dying, to the emergency ward of the Brighton General Hospital. Shaking his head sadly the doctor said, 'The trouble with you, Mr. Hebblethwaite, is you never wear an overcoat.'

With his dying breath, Hebblethwaite responded, 'Well, I do sometimes.'

Adam Curle also tells of Launcelot Batterbury who told his friend, Gwendolyn Fitzbumleigh, that he had mentioned to a colleague that his great-grandfather had been killed at Waterloo.

'And what do you think he said?' Launcelot asked.

'Do tell me,' said Gwendolyn, looking at him with longing.

'He asked which platform. Wasn't that absurd?'

Gwendolyn laughed heartily, 'As if it mattered which platform,' she said, moving a little closer to him.

(Americans need to know that Waterloo, in addition to being the scene of a famous battle, is also a station in the London subway, or 'underground,' as it is called.)

Aristides writes of the English journalist, Jilly Cooper, who discovered that the house she had purchased was reportedly haunted. Her charwoman told her quite earnestly that "the vicar should circumcize it."

Chant of a gathering of liberals:
> "What do you want?"
> "Gradual change!"
> "When do you want it?"
> "In due course."

And on both sides of the Atlantic I've heard about the agnostic, dyslexic insomniac who lay awake all night wondering if there is a Dog.

From Canada comes this reported transcript of an exchange between a US navy vessel and Canadian authorities in Newfoundland:

Canada: Please divert your course 15 degrees South to avoid a collision.

US: Recommend you divert your course 15 degrees North to avoid a collision.

C: Negative. You will have to divert your course 15 degrees to the South to avoid a collision.

US: This is the Captain of a US Navy ship. I say again, divert your course.

C: No. I say again, divert your course.

US: THIS IS THE AIRCRAFT CARRIER USS LINCOLN, THE

SECOND LARGEST SHIP IN THE UNITED STATES' AT-
LANTIC FLEET. WE ARE ACCOMPANIED BY 3 DE-
STROYERS, 3 CRUISERS AND NUMEROUS SUPPORT
VESSELS. I DEMAND THAT YOU CHANGE YOUR
COURSE 15 DEGREES NORTH, I SAY AGAIN, THAT'S
ONE FIVE DEGREES NORTH, OR COUNTER-MEA-
SURES WILL BE UNDERTAKEN TO ENSURE THE SAFE-
TY OF THIS SHIP.

C: This is a lighthouse. Your call.

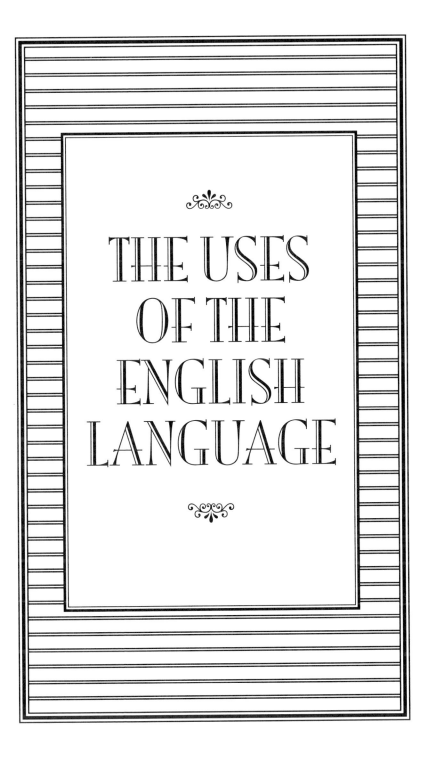

THE USES
OF THE
ENGLISH
LANGUAGE

THE USES OF THE ENGLISH LANGUAGE

Living in Asia for many years I was often struck by the unusual ways things are said by those for whom English is a second language. But I was also made aware of how difficult English is, with its many rules, yet with so many exceptions to those rules. Once in Manila I bought a toothbrush made in Japan. The instructions on the case said:

1) Please clean your tooth 3 times a day
2) After using Tooth Brush please be kept in dry so can be used for long time
3) To use for long time, please avoid to use it in a hot water
4) Is shown in picture, please try to use it for cleaning tooth

Signs seen in the Philippines: Wanted: "Lady Bed Spacers" (university housing for women)

"No Talking on the Hallway" (sign at Union Theological Seminary)

"Doesn't this make your mouth watery?" (written under a painting of spaghetti on a restaurant window)

A Filipino seminarian knocked on the door of registrar Jo Anne Anderson. "I hope I am not molesting you," he said.

A Filipino chapel speaker concluded his sermon on world understanding by saying, "What we need today is more intercourse between people."

A sign on a two-story tailor shop in Hong Kong: "Foreign ladies have fits upstairs"

And a sign in the Hong Kong airport said, "We take your luggage in all directions."

The cafeteria in the Istanbul airport served "terminal soup" while a Chinese restaurant in London offered on its menu "steamed dick with vegetables."

The writer Nino lo Bello in his travels has come across the following signs:

In a Moscow hotel: If this is your first visit to the USSR, you are welcome to it.

In a Budapest hotel: All rooms not denounced by 12:00 will be paid for twicely.

In a Prague travel agency: Take one of our horse- driven city tours – we guarantee no miscarriages.

In a Rumanian hotel: The lift is being fixed for the next days. During that time we regret that you will be unbearable.

I also heard of these notices:

In England: Our establishment serves tea in a bag like mother.

In a Tokyo hotel: The flattening of underwear with pressure is the job of the chambermaid. To get it done, turn her on.
And in Macao an optical establishment has a sign saying you can have your eyes examined while you wait!

In a hotel in Acapulco was this sign: "The manager has personally passed the water served here."

At a dry cleaners in Bangkok: "Drop your pants here for best results."

Near the Precious Blood Church in Nairobi is the Precious Blood Butchery

In Moscow a Russian and I were talking about American literature. He said one of his favorites was *A Tram Called Wish.* It took me a moment to realize he was talking about *A Streetcar Named Desire.*

A BBC commentator called Israel "a mecca for tourists."

Having been invited to speak at a college one winter in northern Sweden, I walked into the auditorium all bundled up. The university president greeted me, then said, "Please take off your clothes."

A helpful reminder to all for whom English is their first language comes from Aristides who wrote (in 'Toys in My Attic,' *American Scholar*, Winter l992):
   "I am very glad that English is the language I grew up in, if only because I don't think I would have had a chance to learn it as an outsider. I am altogether too literal-minded to have been able to accept with serenity its vast number of inconsistencies. Why, any foreigner must wonder, does one drive on the park-

way and park in a driveway? A slim chance and a fat chance – how can these be the same? Drink up, call up, dummy up, slow down, drink it down, play it down, be bored stiff, blue, out of one's gourd, big deal, no deal, do a deal – yumpin' yimminy, bon Dieu, oy gevalt, forget about it!"

I remember my Uncle Walter, who had grown up in Pennsylvania, the son of an immigrant German father and a Scotch-Irish mother, telling about the way the Pennsylvania Dutch spoke when he was boy, saying such things as "Ve grow too soon old and too late schmart." "Make the door shut." "Throw Papa down the stairs his hat." "Throw the cow over the fence some hay." "Ve walk the street down."

It is not only English as a second language that provides hilarity, but it is also the great variety in what we mean by what we say in different countries where English is the first language. For example:

Walter Wink, upon registering one evening at a bed and breakfast in England, was asked by the owner, "When shall I knock you up?"

The English of course are amused when Americans talk about hanging their coats in "the closet." To them that is the water closet, or bathroom, as Americans would say.

An English clergyman preached in an American pulpit and took his text from II Kings: "King Ahab was a good king, but...". His sermon had 3 points:

1) Everyone has a "but"
2) No one can see his own "but"
3) We shouldn't be critical of other people's "buts"

Not realizing that Americans use "butt" to describe one's posterior, he couldn't comprehend the smiles and laughter his sermon brought.

The evangelist E. Stanley Jones once received a letter from Japan that ended with "May the Lord bless and pickle you."

Such things inevitably happen when we try to express ourselves in another language. Garrison Keillor married a Danish woman and moved to Denmark, where he began to learn Danish. He writes, "It's very hard for intelligent persons like us to accept being as stupid as we are in another language. It's frustrating, like becoming a child and remembering how it was to be an adult. You know what you want to say and it won't come out.

"When I went to Denmark, I knew Danish well enough to be able to say things like, 'Good day, my esteemed sausage, it is a pleasure to make the acquaintance of your suitcase and to thank your delightful wife for spending the night with me.' They replied, in perfect English, 'Your Danish is very good.'"

Children and English

What children hear and then write down is often delightfully awry. My wife, who teaches music to elementary school children, especially loves these quotes from children's music essays (as reported by radio station WQXR):

• A virtuoso is a musician with real high morals.

- My very best liked piece is the Bronze lullaby.

- Henry Purcell is a well-known composer few people have ever heard of.

- Handel was half German, half Italian and half English. He was rather large.

- Beethoven wrote music even though he was deaf. He was so deaf he wrote loud music.

- Refrain means don't do it. A refrain in music is the part you better not try to sing.

- I know what a sextet is but I'd rather not say.

When a boy, my son Steve once wrote that he had a "soar throat." It must have been from singing high notes.

One boy came home from school very tired and asked his mother if he had a cliche on his face. "A cliche? What do you mean?" "You know," he said, "a worn-out expression."

Having grown up in West Texas, it amuses me how non-Southerners laugh at the names of some of my Texan class-mates: Billy Bob, Bubba, Mattie Jean, Veda Mae, Veva Gene, Pearlie Mae, Roy Mac, Grover Coy and Rass Elmo.

Jim Forest and Nancy Flier-Forest wrote an anthology of American similies that includes: dead as a doornail; crazy as a loon; mad as a hatter; smart as a whip; ugly as a mud fence; flat as a pancake; stubborn as a mule; dumb as dirt; thin as a rail; cool as a cucumber; naked as a jay bird; deaf as a post; plain as the nose on your face; mad as a hornet.

If clergypersons are defrocked and lawyers disbarred, why aren't electricians delighted, musicians denoted, and cowboys deranged?

Judith Putterman wrote in *The New York Times* of fanciful collective nouns for medical specialists, such as: a throb of cardiologists; a puddle of urologists; a brace of physical therapists; a ganglia of neurologists; a rash of dermatologists; a stitch of plastic surgeons; a vein of vascular surgeons; a clot of hematologists; and a cast of orthopedists.

The greatest book of collective nouns that I am acquainted with is James Lyston's *An Exaltation of Larks* (1991), drawing upon the much earlier work of Dame Juliana Berners' *Book of St. Albans* (1486!). Just a sampling from these books will surely drive you to the source: a gaggle of geese; a parliament of owls; an ostentation of peacocks; a murmuration of starlings; a murder of crows.

Collective religious nouns include: a commentary of rabbis; an om of Buddhists; a transmigration of Hindus; a dreadlock of Rastaferians; a hellfire of fundamentalists; a sobriety of Calvinists; and a glossalalia of Pentecostals. There are also to be found: a fidget of altar boys; a mass of priests; a flap of nuns; an evensong of choirboys; and an immersion of Baptists.

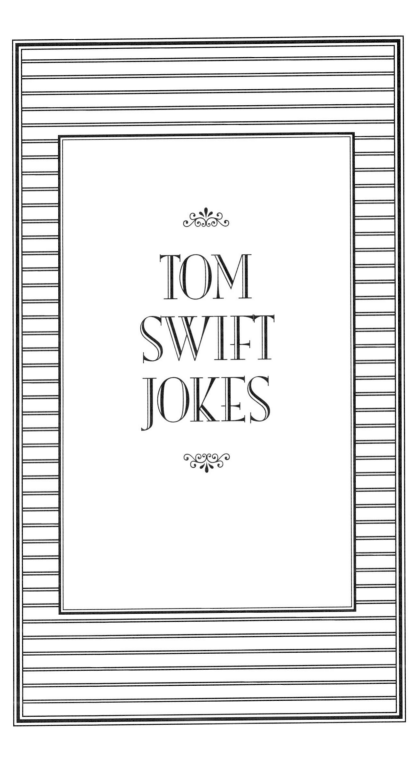

TOM
SWIFT
JOKES

TOM SWIFT JOKES

I first came across Tom Swift jokes in South Korea where Randy and Sue Rice, Presbyterian missionaries, told me about them. Tom Swifties make a delightful use of words having a double meaning. They are easily made up and bring plenty of laughs.

"I've made 3 wrong turns," said Tom forthrightly.

"I'm the new sentry," said Tom guardedly.

"I've dropped my toothpaste," said Tom crestfallen.

"We can seat you now," said Tom unreservedly.

"I'm going to live with Bedouins," said Tom intently.

"I'm going to Londonderry," said Tom airily.

"I work at the cemetery," said Tom gravely.

"I can't find my piano score," said Tom Lizstlessly.

And, of course, it needn't always be Tom Swift:

"I've lost my lamb," said Mary sheepishly.

"That'll be $10," said the customs official dutifully.

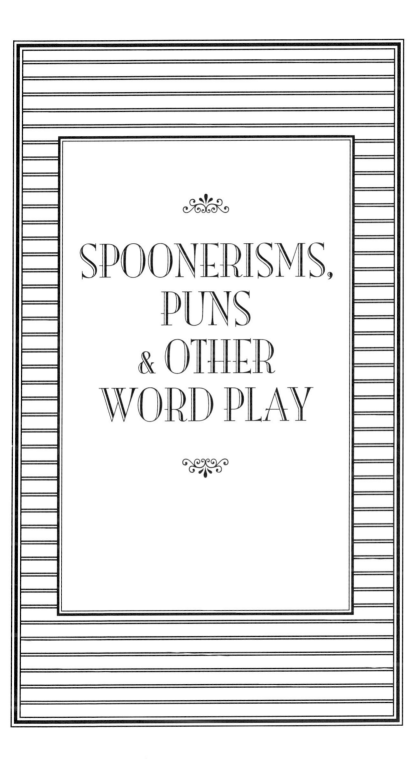

SPOONERISMS, PUNS & OTHER WORD PLAY

SPOONERISMS, PUNS & OTHER WORD PLAY

∽ ∾ ∽ ∾ ∽ ∾ ∽ ∾ ∽ ∾ ∽

William Archibald Spooner was an English clergyman in the early part of this century. His deliberate switching of syllables caused great hilarity, so much that we honor his memory with the label "Spoonerism." He once announced a hymn to be sung as "Kinquering Kongs their Titles Take." He is also credited with referring to "the queer old dean" and the fighter who delivered "a blushing crow."

To those who think punning is the lowest form of humor, F. A. Bather reminds them that William Shakespeare's plays contain 1,062 plays on words, such as the dying Mercutio's describing himself as "a grave man."

The British scholar Walter Redfern tells one of my all-time favorite puns, about the man who goes to a flower shop to get anemones – his wife's favorite flower – for her birthday. The florist has none but persuades him to buy instead a beautiful fern. When the man presents it to his wife he apologizes that he doesn't have her favorite. But she exclaims, "Darling, with fronds like these, who needs anemones?"

Our son Stephen was born in a Seventh Day Adventist Hospital in the Philippines. Although it was a very clean and efficient hospital, they believed in giving numerous enemas to women in labor. After my wife had been given several enemas, I threatened to put up a sign on the door that said, "Friend or Enema?"

The Marx brothers' hilarious antics often were characterized by puns such as this retort of Chico, who, responding to someone who exclaimed, "Eureka!" shot back, "You donna smella so good yourself."

Groucho Marx in the film "Animal Crackers " says that when he shot elephants in Africa he found it very difficult to remove the tusks, but that "in Alabama the Tuscaloosa." He also remarked, "Last night I shot an elephant in my pajamas. How he got there I'll never know."

Groucho said he once attempted to take his daughter swimming but was told that Jews were not allowed. "In that case," quipped Groucho, "can my daughter go in up to her waist? She is only half Jewish."

On Groucho Marx's "You Bet Your Life" quiz show, he asked a young woman why she wasn't married. "I'm waiting for Mr. Right," she answered. "Wilbur or Orville?" asked Groucho. Another contestant with a very heavy accent said he spoke 8 languages. "Which have you been speaking so far?" said Groucho.

S. J. Perelman once said, "I've got Bright's disease and he's got mine." In Perelman's movie "Horse Feathers" Groucho's secretary tells him that Jennings is waxing wroth. "Never mind," says Groucho. "Tell Roth to wax Jennings for a while."

After Walter Winchell praised the opening night of a Broadway show, he added, "Who am I to stone the first cast?"

I love the one about the nun serving tea to the archbishop who said, "How many lords, my lump?" Which reminds me of the true story of Anne Morrow Lindberg's family. Her father was U.S. Ambassador to Mexico. Once they had a famous diplomat to their home for dinner. Mrs. Morrow was quite worried because the man had an enormous nose and she was fearful that the children would say something about it in his presence. Nonetheless the dinner went off perfectly. The children said nothing, nor did they even giggle during dinner. After they were dismissed from the table, the relieved Mrs. Morrow prepared to serve coffee. Turning to the diplomat, she said, "And now, would you like cream in your nose?" This story is often told at the Elizabeth Morrow School in New Jersey where my wife, Jan, teaches.

In the days before television, I listened to the radio often, enjoying comedians such as Red Skelton, Bob Hope, Fibber Magee and Molly, Milton Berle, Jack Benny and Edgar Bergen and Charlie McCarthy. I also remember hearing the stories of bloopers that came across the airwaves, such as

- "the president of the United States, Hoobert Heever"

- "the Duck and Doochess of Windsor"

- "a 21 son galoot"

- "Stay tuned for the sermon, 'Cast your broad upon the waters.' This is the National Breadcasting Company."

Captions for articles are often a delightful source of intended humor. Aristides writes (in 'Toys in My Attic' in *The American Scholar,* Winter 1992) of "When Putsch Comes to Shove," "When Brittania Waves the Rules," "Yes, We Have No Cezannas," and "Days of Whine and Neurosis." And he imagines Gorbachev holding a Kurdish refugee child, with the caption, "Kurd Carrying Communist." In reporting on the ethnic tensions in Czechoslovakia, *US News and World Report*'s by-line for the story was, "No Czech Mates in Slovakia."

I especially like this told me by David O'Leary: Aristotle Onassis wanted to purchase a home in Hollywood. The realtor took him to various homes of the rich and famous. Onassis was photographed looking at the home of the movie actor, Buster Keaton. The next day *The Los Angeles Times'* caption for the photo was, "Aristotle Contemplating the Home of Buster."

Bennett Cerf defined Camelot as "a place to park camels."

I don't know who it was who is reputed to have said when the brilliant Orson Welles walked by, "There but for the grace of God goes God." But it was Leo Froelich who said after watching Nureyev dance, "There but for the God of grace go I."

A certain doctor stopped by her favorite bar every day after work and ordered her favorite drink, an almond daquiri, from her favorite bartender, Dick. It became a routine each afternoon for Dick to get the ingredients ready for the doctor before she arrived. One day he discovered he had no almonds; the only nuts he had were hickory nuts. He thought that she wouldn't even notice the difference so he served her the drink when she came in. She tasted it and said, "Is this an almond daquiri, Dick?" "No," he said, "It's a hickory daquiri, Doc."

Glenn Anderson of Olympia, Washington told this story at the Seabeck Conference of the FOR. A farmer one year raised an enormous strawberry that he felt certain would win a prize in the annual county fair. He called the county agent to come look at it to see what it was worth and if he thought it had a chance of winning first prize. The next day while the farmer was out in the field, the county agent drove up in his pickup, spied the strawberry and went over and began to pull it off the vine. The farmer yelled, "What are you doing? I only asked you to tell me what it was worth." Replied the woman, "I came to seize your berry, not to appraise it."

Quasimodo ("the Hunchback of Notre Dame") was going on vacation so he ran an ad in the Paris newspaper for someone to ring the bells of Notre Dame. The next day there was a knock on the door of his room in the bell tower. He opened the door to find an armless man standing there saying he was applying for the job. "But you can't ring the bells. You have no arms." "I can," said the man, "just give me a chance." "Well," said Quasimodo, "there are the bells. Try if you want." The poor man runs and hits the bells with the side of his face. They ring, but Quasimodo says, "Well, that is all right, but you have to ring them more than once." So the man runs again, hits the bells but falls down and rolls out of the tower onto the pavement below. Quasimodo goes down the stairs and approaches the poor soul just as a policeman arrives on the scene. "Do you know who this is?" asks the policeman. "Well, I don't know his name," says Quasimodo, "but his face rings a bell."

Typographical errors can lead to some hilarious sentences. Long ago my hometown newspaper, *The Big Spring Daily Herald*, reported that "a pedestrian was run over by a pissing automobile." I was once interviewed in the Philippines, and when the article appeared in print the reporter said that "before coming to the Philippines Deats worked a great deal for civil war" (it should have read "civil rights." This was particularly unfortunate as it appeared at a time when there were strong revolutionary stirrings in the islands). Such mistakes are what led the author Isaac Bashevis Singer to write, "An author doesn't die of typhus, but of typos."

Barbara Walters once asked the prolific science fiction writer Isaac Asimov, "What would you do if you only had six months to live?" "Type faster," he replied.

The legendary Samuel Goldwyn was famous for his malapropisms. My favorites are:

- "A verbal agreement isn't worth the paper its written on."

- "If I want your opinion, I'll give it to you."

- "In two words, im possible."

- Leaving on a trip he waved from the boat, "Bon voyage."

- When told to be fair to a competitor who had been an old friend, Goldwyn replied, "We've passed a lot of water under the bridge since then."

A Russian immigrant, referring to New York City, said, "Is total pot of melt."

A flock of geese is flying in a V. The last two birds have a banner between their beaks that says, "Honk if you love geeses."

As the ram runs off the cliff, he says, "I didn't see that ewe turn."

Whenever I am on a beach I always want to throw rocks at the birds because I don't like to leave a tern unstoned.

On my first trip to India I saw a woman in a beautiful native costume. "That's a lovely sarong," I said. "But it isn't a sarong," she said, "it's a sari." "Oh," I replied, "Sari I was sarong."

In Thailand, Mechai Viravayda has an unusual family planning scheme in which policemen in Bangkok distribute condoms on New Year's Eve. He calls it "cops and rubbers."

John Wilkes once said to the Earl of Sandwich, "I predict, sir, that you will one day die, either by hanging or of some loathsome disease."

"Well, that really depends," replied the Earl, "on whether I embrace your principles or your mistress."

The laundryman asks the mother superior at the convent, "Do you have any dirty habits?"

A Basque general and his troops were trapped in a mountain pass and killed. The moral of the story is, "Don't put all your Basques in one exit."

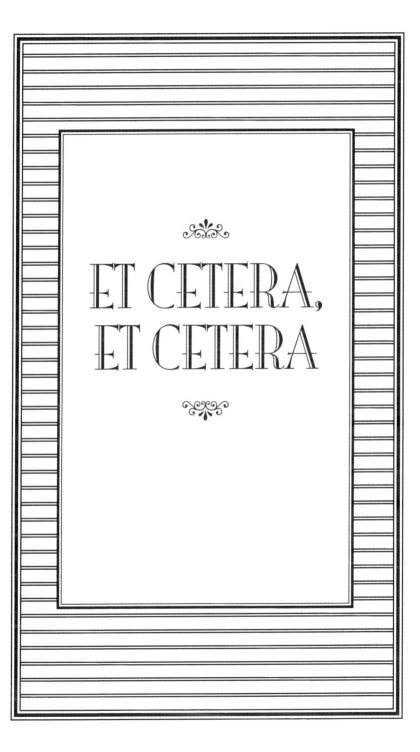

ET CETERA,
ET CETERA

ET CETERA, ET CETERA

Just as the King of Siam, in the musical "The King and I", ended his dictations with "et cetera, et cetera", we come to the end with et cetera, et cetera: some final whimsical and funny stories, humorous bits and pieces of life (some of them even true):

A woman was driving down the New Jersey Turnpike with four penguins in the back seat. A state trooper stopped her and said, "Lady, you'll have to take those penguins to the zoo." "All right, officer," she said and drove off. The next day the same trooper saw the woman in the same car drive by and this time the four penguins were in the back seat wearing sunglasses." Again he stopped her and sternly said, "I thought I told you to take those penguins to the zoo." "I did," she replied, "and today I'm taking them to the beach."

Heil Bollinger told me that when he was in college he fell in love with a woman named Kay. They planned to marry, but one day Heil met a woman named Edith with whom he was also smitten. He was in a deep quandary, being in love with both women. Finally he decided to marry Kay when he realized that he just couldn't have his Kay and Edith too.

Szilagyi Sandor, a linguist from Napoca, Rumania, told me about a musician in the jungle who saw a lion coming toward him. He took out his violin and began playing beautiful music. The lion stopped and sat down to listen. Still others came and did the same until the musician was completely surrounded by lions listening to his music. But then an old lion came up, walked through the others and grabbed the violinist. "Why?" lamented the first lion. "He was playing such beautiful music." "Eh?" asked the old lion, holding up his paw to his deaf ear.

In a similar vein, Cleveland Amory tells the story of a missionary walking in a jungle in Africa when he saw a lion approaching. "O Lord," prayed the missionary, "grant in thy goodness that this lion is a good Christian lion." And then, in the silence that followed, the missionary heard the lion pray, "O Lord, I thank thee for this food which I am about to receive. Amen"

David McReynolds told me about a performance in a Yiddish theater in the old East Side of New York City. The lead actor suddenly collapsed on stage. A doctor came out of the audience and began examining the actor. From the balcony someone yelled, "Give him an enema." The doctor looked up and said, "It won't do any good. He's had a heart attack." The voice from the balcony replied, "It can't hurt."

A man who had a pit bull dog was in a quandary because the dog refused to move when a leash was put on him to go for a walk. The dog simply sat down, so the man just pulled him along the sidewalk. Finally he decided to stop when he realized that he was creating a bottomless pit.

A couple from the US get lost while driving across Canada. They stop and ask a farmer where they are. "Saskatoon, Saskatchewan," he replies. "Gosh," says the driver, "we're more lost than I thought. They don't even speak English here."

A man goes to a psychiatrist, troubled over a recurring dream: one night he is a teepee, the next night he's a wigwam.

The psychiatrist thinks a moment, then says, "It's very obvious. You're too tense."

What does a grape say when you step on it?
Nothing, it just gives a little wine.

One evening a man gives his wife a glass of water and an aspirin. "What is this for?" she asks. "For your headache." "But I don't have a headache," the wife replies. "Gottcha!" says the husband.

Asked to write an inscription on a tombstone, one student wrote, "Bryon, I'm still your mother and I know what you're doing."

The philosopher Descartes went to a bar and ordered a drink. After he finished, the bartender asked if he wanted another one. "I think not," said Descartes—and instantly disappeared.

Dwight Macdonald has defined a foundation as an island of money surrounded by people who want some.

Mark Twain defined a classic as a book which people praise but don't read.

Anne Matthews, noting that four theoretical physicists were specializing in the string theory, said that they might be called 'the String Quartet.'

Germaine Greer said, "Freud is the father of psychoanalysis. It has no mother."

George Bernard Shaw observed that we have not lost our faith, but just transferred it from God to the medical profession.

John Callahan, in a cartoon labeled "A.A. in L.A." shows an agent at a meeting saying, "My name is Mort and I represent Chuck who's an alcoholic."

Coy Nalley, an undertaker in Big Spring, Texas, was a practical joker. Once his friend Roy Cornellison, who owned a cleaning establishment, hired a new assistant. Knowing that Roy went to lunch every day at 12:00, Coy went to the cleaners at 12:15 and told the new assistant that he had been called to repair the cash register, whereupon he picked it up, put it in his car and drove off. When Roy returned from lunch, he was flabbergasted to be told the cash register had been taken—cash and all—by "the repairman." Another time Nalley was on a farm and was told by the farmer that his horse was old and suffering and needed to be shot, but that he(the farmer) just couldn't bring himself to do it. Nalley told him not to worry, that he would do it for him. The next week he and some friends were going dove hunting. When they passed by the farm, Nalley saw the old horse standing by the fence at the road. He told his friends he had always wanted to shoot a horse. He stopped the car, got out, and shot the horse. When he got back in the car, his friends told him he was absolutely crazy.

In Texas some refer to Ft. Worth as the city where "the West begins" and Dallas as the city where "the East peters out." While nationally, Dallas has a cowboy image due to to its football team, the Dallas Cowboys, and the TV show "Dallas," it is more appropriately known as a financial center. Thus when plans were revealed in 1994 of a $9 million bronze sculpture in Dallas depicting a 19th century cattle drive, featuring seventy six-foot steers and three cowboys herding them, one critic said that "a herd of lawyers, bankers and insurance men stampeding through town would be more appropriate (*The New York Times*, January 1, 1994, p. 12)."

Once when Norman Cousins was in the hospital, the nurse gave him a bottle for a urine specimen. When she left, he filled the bottle with apple juice. Upon her return, the nurse remarked with concern that the urine was quite dark. "O.K., I'll run it through again," said Cousins, as he drank the "specimen" from the bottle!

Outside a hotel, Robert Benchley asked a man in fancy uniform to get him a taxi. "My good man, I'll have you to know that I am an admiral," said the uniformed man indignantly. "All right, then," said Benchley, "call me a battleship."

My friend Lennie Leonetti answered the phone at home. "You have the wrong number," he told the caller. The stranger was undeterred. "How do you know this is the wrong number?" said the insistent caller. "Have I ever lied to you?" said Lennie.

Another friend, Pat Williams, who has three brothers, found out in grade school how babies are conceived. When she came home she told her mother what she had heard and wanted to know if that was true. "Well, yes," her embarrassed mother replied. Pat was indignant. "You mean you let daddy do that to you four times?!" she asked.

A couple from the Midwest was driving through Vermont. The husband remarked that in 20 miles they'd be in Calais, using the French pronunciation, "Cal-ay." His wife corrected him, saying it was pronounced "Callas" in Vermont. Unable to agree, they stopped for coffee when they reached the town. "Excuse me," said the husband to the waitress, "How do you pronounce the name of this place?" Very slowly she replied, "Dunkin' Donuts."

A herring and a whale developed a very close friendship and were always seen swimming around together. One day they had a falling out and both swam off in opposite directions. A dolphin, surprised to see the herring swimming all by himself, asked where his friend was. "How should I know?" replied the herring. "Am I my blubber's kipper?"

A very rich snail went into a Nissan showroom and told the salesperson he wanted to buy a 280 Z sportscar. Furthermore he wanted it to be bright red, and to have air bags and the best tape deck available. Finally, he said that he wanted the 'Z' on the fenders to be changed to an 'S.' "Well," said the salesperson, "that would be extremely expensive as it would have to be handcrafted and that is a very costly process." "Cost is no object," replied the snail, "please order the change." The arrangements were made and two weeks later the car was ready: bright red, air bags, expensive tape deck and the handcrafted 'S' on the fenders. The rich snail came in, paid cash for the car, got in the driver's seat and prepared to drive away. "I am just curious," said the salesperson, "would you please tell me why you wanted to change the 'Z' to an 'S' on the fenders?" "Of course," said the snail. "I just thought it would be great to go down the highway and have people look at me and say, "Wow! Look at that S car go."

During a performance John Barrymore called out, "A horse! A horse! My Kingdom for a horse!" Someone in the balcony laughed, whereupon Barrymore strode forward, looked up and exclaimed, "Ho, saddle yon braying ass!"

George Burns says that the good thing about living to 100 is that very few people die after 100.

Robert Louis Stevenson muses, "One person I have to make good: myself. But my duty to my neighbor is much more nearly expressed by saying that I have to make him happy if I may."

Keep fightin' for
freedom and justice, beloveds,
but don't you forget
to have fun doin' it.
Lord, let your laughter
ring forth.

– MOLLY IVINS

The message of peace
is far too serious
to be left to anyone but
clowns, artists and mystics.
Travel in their company.

– MARY LOU KOWNACKI, OSB

RICHARD DEATS is on the national staff of the U.S. Fellowship of Reconciliation. Author, public speaker and workshop leader, he has travelled throughout the world working for peace and justice. He is also the author of a biography *Martin Luther King, Jr.: Spirit-Led Prophet.* He and his wife, Jan, have four children and twelve grandchildren.

The Fellowship of Reconciliation, begun in 1914 and now at work in over forty countries, is composed of women and men who recognize the essential unity of all creation and have joined together to explore the power of love and truth for resolving human conflict. Inquiries for more information are welcomed.